THE MIDNIGHT THIEF

THE MIDNIGHT THIEF

SYLVIA BISHOP

Illustrated by
Flavia Sorrentino

SCHOLASTIC

Published in the UK by Scholastic, 2021
Euston House, 24 Eversholt Street, London, NW1 1DB
Scholastic Ireland, 89E Lagan Road, Dublin Industrial Estate,
Glasnevin, Dublin, D11 HP5F

ISBN 978 0702 30148 3

A CIP catalogue record for this book
is available from the British Library.

Printed by CPI Group (UK) Ltd, Croydon, CR0 4YY
Paper made from wood grown in sustainable forests
and other controlled sources.

1 3 5 7 9 10 8 6 4 2

www.scholastic.co.uk

For my nephew and godson, Wilbur John,

with love and astonishment

Anyone who has spent some
time in an enclosed space with
an excited bat knows what it is to
encounter a fundamentally alien
form of life.

—THOMAS NAGEL,
"What Is It Like to Be a Bat?"

The bat that changed everything

Freya was in the school attic when she found the bat. It was a very ordinary sort of bat, but it was about to change everything, whether it wanted to or not.

She didn't know that it was a change-everything bat at the time, of course. It took her a moment to realize it was a bat at all. It was hunkering on top of a pile of papers, a little lump of fur without legs or arms or obvious head, its wings folded up and clamped at its sides like spears.

She almost screamed, but she held herself back. At Throgmorton's School for Girls, the attics were out of

1

bounds, so screaming would be a very stupid thing to do.

Besides, she felt a flicker of kinship with the bat. Freya's dad always said she could make friends with a crocodile. It was true. For Freya, everyone and everything was a friend she hadn't made yet.

"Hello, bat," she said.

The bat twitched uncertainly.

"It's OK," said Freya, crouching down. "I won't hurt you. I can keep a secret."

The bat stayed very still, in a secretive sort of way.

"How did you get in?" Freya whispered. "You weren't here yesterday." She resisted the urge to reach out and stroke the furry little body. "I'm new too. I'd fly away if I were you – it's not a great place. I'm here because of some dragons. Cool, huh?"

But before the bat could offer an opinion on this strange claim, the attic door banged open and Abigail Langford stuck her head round. "Miss *Henderson!*" she crowed. "She's in the *attic!*"

After that it was pandemonium.

Freya took an instinctive step away from the door,

tripped over a globe and fell into a tower of books, which tumbled and thudded and crashed to the ground, smashing a couple of glass vials on the way. (The school's founder, Lord Joseph Edward Throgmorton the First, had been a keen scientist and explorer; the attic was full of all sorts of mysterious scientific instruments and leather-bound books and maps and cases full of rocks and ... well, and lots of things that make a crash when you knock them over.)

All the commotion was too much for the bat, which shook open its wings and began skitter-flapping about – left then right then up then left again, bobbing about like a ship in a storm. Frantically, it began tacking towards the door. This horrified Abigail, who screamed and stumbled backwards over a pile of books and papers. She went tumbling down the stairs, into Miss Henderson, the headmistress, who went tumbling with her, closely followed by the papers and books and a lot of dust.

Freya couldn't see this, of course – she was still lying on the floor – but she could hear enough to guess that things were not going well. She sneezed, and shut her eyes.

Below, the flapping receded. As Freya lay there, a distant and growing babble of voices suggested that some kind of bat hunt was assembling. She felt bad. She hadn't kept her secret very well guarded.

She sneezed again, a defeated sort of sneeze, then once more with determination. She had her dad's bunch of keys in her blazer pocket, which she kept with her for luck and courage, and she gave them a squeeze as she sneezed a fourth time. By the fifth and final sneeze she was upright, eyes open, dusting herself off. She didn't know why the headmistress had been looking for her, and it was very unlikely to be good news, but there was no sense lying here in the dust waiting to find out. She took a deep breath and headed to the stairs, and the world below.

As she walked down the hallway towards the babble, Henny came round the corner towards her. Henny was the headmistress's sister – so her real name was Miss Henderson, too, but no one called her that – and she taught science. She was quite a brilliant scientist, in her own way, but also a walking disaster. Legend had it that decades ago she had tried to make a novel kind of engine which didn't need any petrol to run; unfortunately it *did* need something called nitroglycerine, which had resulted in her accidentally blowing up half the school's lab, and very neatly blowing off her own eyebrows in the process. Freya found this legend very easy to believe.

As Henny half ran down the corridor now, cardigan agape, Freya was struck by how much she looked like a bat. A worried bat, with lilac chunky-knit wings.

"Oh dear, Freya," she panted. "A bat! In the school! I have to find a *bucket*. Oh dear."

"Good luck!" said Freya.

"Oh *dear*," agreed Henny, smiling at her vaguely, and flapping away up the attic stairs. Freya kept going.

A door to her right opened, and a face appeared, eyes narrowed: Abigail's best friend, Zara.

"Abigail hurt her ankle and you are in so much trouble," Zara hissed.

Freya wanted to say that she hadn't *asked* Abigail to come up to the attic and sneak on her. But she was more interested in finding the bat than in arguing. So she kept walking, saying nothing.

Around the corner, she found more chaos. The bat was backed up against a wall, still flapping about in panic. Mrs Clod, the caretaker, was jabbing towards it with a broom for no obvious reason, while a cluster of girls in grey-and-black uniform watched in fascination. The history teacher, Miss Richards, was on the phone, trying to make herself heard. The headmistress, Miss Henderson, was nowhere to be seen.

Watching the bat's panic was horrible. "Mrs Clod," said Freya, "you're frightening it."

Mrs Clod nodded, and jabbed again.

"I think it's just an average-sized bat," Miss Richards was saying into the phone. "No, smaller than that, and brownish . . . yes, of course." She gave Mrs Clod a pained look. "Mrs Clod, please. We're not trying to *kill* the poor thing."

Mrs Clod seemed deeply puzzled by this information. She paused and looked at her broom in confusion.

More girls were joining the gaggle of watchers, giggling and squealing. The scene began to feel to Freya like a fever dream. Mrs Clod went back to jabbing fruitlessly in the direction of the bat; Henny arrived with a bucket, breathing heavily, and promptly tripped over the telephone cord; Miss Featherly, the English teacher, appeared suddenly at Freya's left shoulder and declaimed, *"Like a glove, a black glove thrown up at the light, and falling back. . ."*

Miss Featherly liked to quote poetry without warning or explanation. She looked around at the girls for a response now, hands clasped to her large pearl necklace, her willowy body swaying slightly with emotion.

Everyone ignored her, except Freya, who said "Oh" to be nice – although to be honest she found Miss Featherly a bit much.

"D. H. Lawrence, 'Bat'," said Miss Featherly. "Wonderful."

"Sorry, yes, I'm still here," said Miss Richards into the phone. "Someone tripped over the cord. When can you come for the bat?"

"Oh dear, I've brought a bucket," announced Henny.

Then Mrs Clod took the bucket and, with astonishing speed, slammed it over the bat and against the wall. Or more accurately, against a floor-to-ceiling portrait of Lord Throgmorton, so that His Lordship now appeared to have a bucket for a head. Henny, trembling, approached with a lid to slide over the top. Everybody held their breath as the two of them lowered the sealed bucket, bat inside.

"*Wings like bits of umbrella*," quoth Miss Featherly, in hushed tones. "Beautiful."

In the bucket, the bat was scrabbling and flapping and thudding. But it was no use. It was over.

Except, of course, that a whole lot of other secrets were about to fly free. So it wasn't really over at all – for the humans at Throgmorton's, it was just beginning. But this didn't make the bat any less unhappy.

What was all this like for the bat?

That's a difficult question. Bats "echolocate", which means they make a very high sound – too high for humans to hear – and then they listen to how that sound echoes off the objects around them. That way, they can work out the shape and size and distance of everything nearby, in perfect detail. That's why they can "see" in the dark – it isn't really seeing at all. It's echolocating.

It is mind-bogglingly difficult for humans to imagine what this might be like. It's so difficult that a man called Thomas Nagel wrote a whole essay on the question, called "What Is It Like to Be a Bat?", which was printed in a very clever journal and read by lots of very clever people. And his conclusion was, in short: "Not a clue."

But we can probably assume that it's lonely to echolocate inside a bucket, and just get bucket echoes back, and nothing else.

It must be a bit like darkness.

Throgmorton's School for Girls

With the bat safely contained, Throgmorton's School for Girls shook itself, and settled back down to a regular evening.

First Miss Richards and Mrs Clod departed, bucket held proudly aloft. Henny flapped her cardigan at the girls, in a way that was probably meant to convey an instruction, then hurried after them.

Miss Featherly wafted a bejewelled hand dramatically, declaring, *"Black piper on an infinitesimal pipe."* She looked around for appreciation. Finding none, she sailed off with dignity to appreciate herself somewhere else.

The girls took a little longer to settle, still rippling from the disturbance. But then the bell went for dinner, so at last they broke off into their usual twos and threes and drifted away to the dining hall.

Freya had been at the school for over a month now, but she still didn't have a usual two or three. In fact, the others would hardly speak to her. They didn't have anything against her – they didn't even know her. But Abigail, the head girl, didn't like her; and nobody wanted to be on the wrong side of Abigail Langford. So Freya went down to the dining hall alone, as usual.

The walk to the dining hall was a strange one. The school had been Lord Throgmorton's home when he was alive, and it was more like a castle than a normal school. Freya made her way through grey stone hallways lit by lanterns, lined with tapestries and statues and endless portraits of Lord Throgmorton the First. The way those halls twisted and turned made the school feel like a maze.

It *should* have been a beautiful, curious place, but it felt to Freya as though it had somehow been hollowed out. The softly lit stone walls did not match

the unsettling emptiness they now housed, always too orderly and too cold and too quiet.

In the dining hall, two hundred girls stood waiting at the long tables. At the far end stood the mistresses. Freya slipped into her place just in time to avoid a demerit for tardy behaviour.

Miss Henderson was not there. It was Miss Richards instead who cleared her throat and said: "Welcome, girls. No notices this evening. Time for the school song!

When you're ready, Miss Timms."

At the piano, Miss Timms, ever ready, struck up the chords of the school song. The Throgmorton Trust, who looked after Lord Throgmorton's legacy, insisted that this was sung every night; it wasn't really a proper school song, just a list of all the places His Lordship had built in the city. Freya joined in, without much enthusiasm:

> *Happy, glad and proud are we,*
> *Lord Throgmorton's girls to be!*
> *Founder of our seat of learning*
> *To be like him is our yearning.*
> *Seven gifts he left behind*
> *For the curious of mind:*
> *His Museum and Library*
> *House wonders for the world to see!*
> *His two Schools, for girls and boys*
> *Fill young minds with wisdom's joys.*
> *There's a Theatre and a Church*
> *We shall not his name besmirch.*

(Freya always thought that line was a low point. It rhymed with church well enough, but it didn't seem to have much to do with the rest of the song.)

> *And for life's illumination*
> *The Society for Science, Invention and Exploration.*

(This line did not scan at all well, and you had to sing it very fast to make it fit. Henny always sang it extra loudly. She adored the Society, and it was an open secret that she was desperate to work there instead of at the school.)

> *May we show our gratitude*
> *Daily with our attitude:*
> *Seek to learn, and to obey,*
> *Be clean and good in every way.*

(This was the only line Mrs Clod ever sang, in her surprisingly melodious bellow.)

> *Happy, glad and proud are we*

Miss Timms played some rousing chords at the end to make up for the lacklustre singing, and then at last they were allowed to sit and eat. There was a clattering of two hundred chairs as two hundred girls sat down to two hundred waiting plates of half-cold shepherd's pie.

Freya's mind was still on the bat, and the frantic way it had flapped inside the bucket. She barely noticed the pie.

"What do you think'll happen to the bat?" she asked Quiet Carol. Carol was painfully shy, but Freya was good with shy people, and Carol would sometimes talk to her. But this time Carol just stared extra hard at her pie and flushed furiously. Which, Freya guessed, probably meant that Abigail was coming.

Sure enough, the head girl was limping towards her, ponytail swinging. She was leaning on her best friend, Zara, with the general air of someone who may never walk again. The two of them halted righteously at Freya's seat.

"Miss Henderson wants to see you after dinner,"

said Abigail.

"OK," said Freya. "Is your ankle all right?"

Abigail ignored this. "We aren't allowed in the attics," she went on. "School rule two hundred and sixty-three – that's a class-three rule. You'll get at *least* four demerits."

Throgmorton School had a labyrinthine system of rules, which translated into demerits, which translated into punishments when they were added up at the end of the week. All the students were given a copy of the Complete and Updated Book of Rules, but it was very boring, so Freya had given up trying to understand how it all worked. Demerits were just something that happened to her, like weather.

"Just because your dad's a so-called *celebrity*," spat Abigail, "doesn't mean you can break the rules, you know. Come on, Zara." And the two of them wheeled round, a little awkwardly, and marched back to their own seats.

Freya was used to Abigail's comments about her dad, so she ignored this. Dr Robinson *wasn't* a celebrity. He was an archaeologist, and he was employed by the Throgmorton Museum. Freya used to travel with him from dig to dig, getting her lessons from him in the evenings.

But that part of her life was over now. Over the last decade, her dad had spent as much time as he could tracking down seven ivory statuettes: the Eldrida Dragons. They were famous in Anglo-Saxon legend, but no one had been sure that they existed. On finding the seventh and last, he had won the Throgmorton Trust's Lifetime Service Award, which was a very big deal. It was only given out once a decade. And on top of that he was presented with a beautiful set of seven silver keys that opened the seven Throgmorton buildings, an honour which no one had been given for a *century*. He also got the usual prize, namely, a lot of money. Only instead of taking the money, he asked for it to be sent straight to the school, to pay for Freya to have a Proper Education.

Freya had thought she *was* having a proper education. But he had been worried about her schooling for a long time, and Throgmorton's was a very famous school, known for hiring mistresses who were experts in their subjects: Miss Richards had even published papers on the Eldrida Dragons herself, and Miss Featherly published poetry, and Miss Timms wrote music, and Henny – well – mostly blew things up, but in an impressive sort of way.

So his heart was set on it. And besides, the books Freya had read made boarding school sound quite fun. It mostly seemed to involved midnight feasts, featuring lots of condensed milk.

This had not, so far, been accurate.

The Throgmorton Trust had agreed to the plan, and instructed the headmistress to give Freya the best room in the school. This meant she had a room all to herself, with a beautiful old fireplace and a window seat overlooking the grounds.

Unfortunately, before Freya arrived, this had been Abigail's room. When Freya had found this out she had immediately asked to swap back, because it *was* unfair, but Miss Henderson had refused. And now Abigail hated her. Miss Henderson, who everyone knew had been hoping for the prize money herself, seemed to hate her too. It had been hard settling in, with the head girl *and* the headmistress against her.

There was going to be a big party at the school in Freya's dad's honour in four days' time. On the plus side, this meant she would get to see him. On the down side, all the fuss made Abigail even more furious – and the headmistress, too.

The headmistress. Freya wondered just how much trouble she was going to be in this time, and she squeezed the luck-and-courage keys again trying not to mind too much. These were the seven silver keys her dad had won for his prize. He had left them behind by mistake, and when he realized, he had written to Freya from his latest dig and asked her to hand them in to Miss Henderson, to be kept safe. But she didn't want to. They were all she had left of him. She told anyone who asked that he'd given them to her on purpose.

"Good luck with Miss Henderson, Freya," whispered Quiet Carol.

"Thanks," said Freya, smiling at her. Carol was quite overcome by this, and ate the rest of her dinner in silence.

At last, the bell rang for the end of dinner. Two hundred chairs clattered, and four hundred feet stampeded from the dining hall, out into the entrance hall, where Freya paused.

The entrance hall was cavernous, lit by lanterns hanging from a long wooden beam overhead, beyond which the roof rose to a vaulted point. In the centre, on a shiny new plinth, there was a small ivory statue of a Dragon.

Freya stopped to look at it, even though it made her heart hurt a bit. It had been covered in mud when her father had first held it up to her in triumph. Now it sat demurely in a glass case, cleaned  and polished, with three big locks on it to be triple safe. (Mrs Clod liked putting locks on things. At first it had just had one, but when Miss Richards had given them all an assembly on the legend of the Dragons and their infamous curse, she had added two more to be safe. She refused to go near the Dragon now.)

"Hope you're OK in there," said Freya.

The Dragon looked back at her with blank ivory

eyes.

Freya squeezed the luck-and-courage keys once more, then tapped across the entrance hall, footsteps echoing. At Miss Henderson's door, she hesitated.

Her dad had said she could make friends with a crocodile, and it was probably true; but even Freya didn't want to make friends with Miss Henderson.

Still, she had been summoned. She knocked, and the voice inside said "Enter!"

She entered.

The headmistress was standing behind her desk. She had her sister's staring eyes, and a squat little body which perched oddly on her long limbs, wrapped in silks and softly chinking silver jewellery. The effect was overwhelmingly *spidery*. She was nursing a glass of something dark brown, and every time she took a sip, she licked her top lip with her small pink tongue.

For three sips-and-licks she regarded Freya in silence. Freya stood awkwardly, feeling like an untidy blot on the office. At last the headmistress said, "Sit."

Freya sat. In the corner of the room, the bat was hurling itself at the top of the bucket with a sickening *thlop* sound.

"The attic," said Miss Henderson – sip, lick – "is forbidden to students. You know that?"

"Yes, Miss Henderson."

"There is a bat in the school. Abigail is injured. I am injured. I am supposed to have already left for a particularly lovely little hotel in Sodden-Under-Foot, where I will be attending the Annual Conference for Outstanding Headmistresses tomorrow, and instead I am *still here* sorting out this *outrage*, and I will be leaving *very late*." Her breast heaved with the passion of this list of grievances; then she took a deep breath, and regained her composure. "The trouble you are capable of causing, Freya, is impressive for one small child."

Freya had learned that "Sorry, Miss Henderson" was the safest response to any list of accusations, so she said it. But she got the impression she hadn't sounded sorry enough or small enough when she said it, because Miss Henderson continued to glare. *Thlop, thutter*, went the bucket.

"At the time of your trespass," Miss Henderson went on, "I had been looking for you, in order to discuss *this*." She held up a letter.

Freya recognized it at once. She had written it shortly after she arrived – she knew better now.

"*Dear Miss Henderson*," the headmistress read, in a high-pitched imitation of Freya's voice. "*I am writing to ask whether I could start a football club on Saturdays.*"

On Saturday mornings, every girl at Throgmorton's attended a club. They could choose from a list, but they all had to do *something*. There hadn't been a football club when Freya arrived, and she loved football, so she had made a suggestion. Now she knew that suggestions were frowned upon.

"*I have a ball in my suitcase,*" went on Miss Henderson, "*and we could use the lacrosse pitch.*" She put down the letter. "Well, how marvellous, Freya. To think, for decades Throgmorton's girls have been winning trophies in lacrosse, and all this time we were just waiting for someone to arrive and graciously offer us the gift of *football*."

She had to lick her lips three times to recover from this speech. Whenever the headmistress spoke, Freya felt as though each sentence was like a spider shooting silk, building a web around an unsuspecting fly. The safest thing was not to wriggle.

"Well?" said Miss Henderson. "Do you have anything to say for yourself?"

"I just thought—" Freya began – and knew immediately this was a mistake. Whenever her dad had come home in the evenings, he used to give her a hug and say, "Hello, little one. What are you thinking about?" And whether it was the ancient Greeks or what to have for dinner, he would really want to know about it. But at Throgmorton's, no one seemed to want Freya to think *anything*.

She was saved from finishing her sentence by a knock on the door, and Miss Richards poked her head round. Freya quite liked the history mistress. She didn't mind too much if you thought things, and she always wore interesting jewellery with old Anglo-Saxon designs, and taught them things in her classes which even Freya didn't know. But she was very proper and teacher-ish, and it felt as though her most interesting side was always tidied away: her long auburn hair was tidied up into a serious bun, and her face was tidied up into a sensible expression.

She nodded at Freya, then said, "Miss Henderson, the man from the wildlife conservation trust is here. Mr Stone."

"Conservation trust?" Miss Henderson frowned. "I asked you to call pest control."

"I did. They said bats aren't pests, and the conservation trust were the right people to ask, in case the bat was injured."

"Fine, fine, show him in."

"One other thing. He's brought his children."

Miss Henderson reached for her glass. "What on earth for?"

"Well, it's the evening, and last minute, so he hadn't made arrangements..."

The headmistress wafted this away with her hand.

"Fine. Show him in, the children can wait outside. Freya, you're dismissed. For your trespass, I will be adding six demerits to your weekly total, and two more for your insolent letter. I think we can assume that desserts and weekend outings will be off the cards for some time. If this carries on, Freya, I will have no choice but to call your father."

Freya got up to go, as Miss Richards showed in a small bespectacled man. He smiled happily at her, unaware that she was in disgrace and not to be smiled at.

She slipped out into the entrance hall, leaving the three of them to it. She had expected the demerits, and didn't really care; but the threat to call her dad rattled her. She really didn't want him to know that she was doing badly. It was the only reason she still kept to the more pointless school rules – when she could remember what they were. She breathed deeply, once – twice – three times. And then a voice came from up above her, up amongst the lanterns, and she nearly choked on all those deep breaths in surprise.

"Hello," it said. "Are you all right?"

While Freya was looking up, Miss Henderson was spidering away at Mr Stone. Mr Stone quickly stopped listening, and watched the actual spider on the bush outside her window instead.

The spider was doing something very clever. She was moving about on tiptoe, feeling the invisible forces of the universe with the hairs on her feet.

Everything in the universe – even you – has an invisible force around it, which pulls some things closer, and pushes other things away. This is called an electric field.

Because of electric fields, a leaf and a spider's silk will push each other away a little bit. And because of electric fields, air and a spider's silk will pull towards each other a little bit.

The spider was feeling for somewhere with a strong push, and a strong pull. When she found it, she put out a line of silk, and the leaf pushed it away and the air pulled it closer – and she was lifted right off the bush, and floated away, like a tiny eight-legged balloon.

Miss Henderson did not float off anywhere, to Mr Stone's deep regret.

The twins

Freya stared upwards at the speaker. For a mad moment, she thought she was seeing another bat. But it wasn't a bat: it was a boy. His black coat flapped about as he hung upside down by his knees from the beam, as though it was monkey bars.

There was a girl next to him in the same pose, and a matching black coat. They both had enormous spectacles, which dangled from their necks on string as they hung there. The girl's pair were sellotaped in two places. Freya wondered how many times you had to break your glasses before someone tied them to you with string.

"Why were you in the headmistress's room? Were you being told off?" said the boy. "It feels like you might get told off for *anything* in here. It's all solemn and quiet. Is it horrible? That Miss Richards woman seemed nice though. Is she nice?"

"Um," said Freya, trying to keep up. She was distracted by the girl's dangerous rocking back and forth. "Yes, I was. It is a bit. She's OK. Are you sure that's...?" But she wasn't sure how to end that question. The children swung upside down with total nonchalance.

"Safe?" suggested the boy. "Yes. We like being upside down. Don't we, Esmie?"

The girl nodded, which looked odd while she was

hanging that way. Her forehead wagged like a chin, and her hair flapped about like a beard.

"I'm Daniel," said the boy. "And this is Esmie. We're twins. We're here about the bat; our dad knows all about bats and he works for a charity that looks after animals, and we help. Did you see the bat? What's your name?"

"Freya," said Freya, "and yes. It was me who found it."

"Oh!" said Daniel. And in a flash of stomach-fluttering movement, he swung himself upright, crawled along the beam, and shimmied down at the other end. Esmie didn't join him, but she blinked down from above with added interest.

"Where did you find it?" said Daniel. "It's *very* strange for a bat to be awake in winter. Did it seem all right? How long had it been awake, d'you reckon? Bats should be asleep saving energy, 'cause there isn't any food, and if they wake up and can't find food they might die. Did it seem hungry? Was it hurt?"

"I found it in the attic. I . . . I don't know if it was all right. I don't know how to tell."

On the ground, Daniel was significantly shorter

than Freya, although she thought probably about the same age. He had put his glasses on, and he looked up at Freya so intensely with his huge eyes that she suddenly felt very ashamed of her failure to accurately judge the emotional state of a bat.

"It wasn't making any noise," she offered.

"It would have been," said Daniel. "But you wouldn't have heard it, 'cause it's ultrasonic."

"Er," said Freya. "Ultrawhat?"

"You explain it, Esmie," said Daniel.

"Ultrasound is sound that's too high for humans to hear," Esmie said; then she was silent once more.

"Other animals can hear it," continued Daniel, "but our ears aren't good enough. Bats make ultrasonic noises and then they listen to them bouncing off things to find out what's there, and that's called echolocating. Isn't that cool? Humans have made machines to do the same thing and it's called sonar. But we're not as good at it as bats. They're really precise. And really loud."

Freya had a lot of questions about this, but Daniel had moved on, and didn't pause to hear them. He had wandered over to the Dragon as he spoke. "We heard about these. Dad says they're worth a fortune. I was expecting them to be gold or something." He considered the statuette. "It's sort of ugly, don't you think? What's it made of?"

"It's just ivory," said Freya. "But they're really old – Anglo-Saxon. They're the *Eldrida Dragons*."

She waited, but this did not produce any effect on the twins. It was strange to Freya that people could simply have not heard of the Eldrida Dragons. It had been her dad's life mission to find all seven, and Freya had known about them for as long as she could remember. The legends of ancient Britain were her bedtime stories. But to everyone else, they were just funny lumps of ivory. Only Miss Richards really understood how special they were. The Anglo-Saxons were her speciality, and she had thrown out all of her usual lesson plans to teach the girls ancient British legends instead, in the Dragons' honour.

"What's so special about them?" Daniel said.

It was difficult to know where to start. "They're *legendary*. They're meant to ward off evil, and there was one for each of the seven Anglo-Saxon kingdoms,

33

given to them by this woman called Eldrida. She was sort of like a witch." Freya joined Daniel in front of the Dragon. "That one's the Dragon of Mercia. The marks on it are runes, they make a sort of spell. This rune here is for ill health – that one's famine – that's demons – and this one is a sort of 'keep out' sign. . ."

Daniel blinked at the ugly little statuette with slightly more respect. "*Cool*. Where are the other six?"

"In the other Throgmorton buildings. They're meant to be kept separate so that no one can have all their power."

"Says who?"

"Says the curse. It's the most famous thing about them: in all the old legends, whenever anyone tried to keep them together, the seven guardian spirits awoke to enact revenge." She pulled a gruesome face, which made Esmie laugh overhead, and added, "People got sick and died in fires and all sorts."

Daniel looked very serious. He turned back to the Dragon with added respect.

Freya didn't believe in the curse, but the stories were fun. Henny had got very excited when she heard them, and she wanted to examine the school's statue to see if there was a Scientific Explanation for the way they made people ill and caused things to burst into flame and so on; but she was under *strict* instructions from Miss Henderson not to touch it. For once, Freya agreed with the headmistress. She didn't want the Dragons going the same way as Henny's exploding engine.

Daniel opened his mouth with the air of someone who had about eighty-three more questions. But just then, they were interrupted by Mr Stone opening the office door.

He smiled at them all. If it bothered him that Esmie was currently hanging from the ceiling, he didn't let it show. "Daniel, Esmie," he said, "I've got some paperwork to finish up here. Would you take the bat for me? It seems perfectly well. We can release it safely."

Daniel came forward for the bucket. Esmie swung herself upright and began her descent.

"The headmistress," said Mr Stone, "would like it released no less than five miles from the school grounds."

"But then it will get confused, and—" Daniel began.

"She has been very insistent," said Mr Stone, a little

wearily. "It seems she was expecting some sort of pest control. I said we'd do our best. So maybe you and Esmie could just – *pop it in the car.*"

A look passed between father and son which Freya couldn't quite read, then Daniel took the bucket. Mr Stone retreated, and shut the door.

"Want to see it go?" Daniel offered, turning to Freya. "You found it."

"OK," said Freya. "I'm not really meant to leave the school, but I can go a couple of minutes without anyone noticing. Where's your car?"

Daniel and Esmie exchanged glances, Esmie now mercifully the right way up. Daniel leaned close to Freya. "We don't have a car," he whispered. "We're not releasing the bat that far away, it'll get confused and lost. It needs to find its way home. Is there somewhere here we can release it without your headmistress seeing?"

Freya felt a rush of affection for this strange bat family who acted like Miss Henderson was just another human, and not queen of the universe. She nodded. "Follow me."

She led them round twists of hallway to the back

door, and out into the gardens. These were probably beautiful in summer. Now, in mid-November, skeleton trees ruled over a kingdom of mulched leaves and dank puddles. CLIMBING IS PROHIBITED: TWO DEMERITS, said the signs on the trees. NO SITTING IDLY BY THE POND, said another sign, ONE DEMERIT. A third, next to some thorns, declared, THE ROSES ARE NOT FOR SMELLING.

They squelched across the garden, keeping to the deeper shadows in the darkness. Freya envied the twins their thick black coats; she was shivering in her blazer. The shivering made the keys in her pocket jangle.

As they walked, Daniel kept up a stream of questions about school. Freya answered them as best she could, but the questions came so fast that she could hardly draw breath. She told him about her dad's big prize and her arrival here, and the cruelty of the headmistress and Abigail and the silent wall of the other girls and the Complete and Updated Book of Rules and the bland-lukewarm-never-quite-enough-ness of the food which did not, it turned out, include condensed milk at midnight.

"I'm not explaining it very well," she said.

"Oh, you are," said Daniel. "It's just that I ask too many questions."

Then Esmie broke her silence, which surprised Freya so much that she almost lost her footing on the mulch. "It sounds bad," she said. "You don't deserve to be treated like that."

Freya felt a bit of a lump in her throat, and she didn't really know what to say to that. She squeezed her keys, but the lump didn't go away.

They had reached the wall that ran around the gardens, high grey stone, casting a thick layer of extra shadow. "Will here be all right?" Freya said.

"Perfect." Daniel set the bucket on the ground and crouched down. He pulled the lid back an inch and peered inside. "Esmie! I think it's Moriarty."

As Esmie pulled out a notebook and wrote something down, Daniel explained, "We know the bats in this city pretty well. This one's from the Science Society Roost. We call him Moriarty."

Freya squatted down next to him. "Hello, Moriarty," she said. "Pleasure to make your acquaintance."

"Ready to say goodbye?" asked Daniel. "He'll fly out fast."

"Yes. I guess." Freya felt an unexpected ache. "I know it's stupid when I hardly knew him, but – he really felt like *mine*. Like a friend, sort of."

Esmie blinked knowingly, and Daniel said, "Yeah, we know that feeling. Bats are like that. But you can't keep them." He sighed. "Still," he added, "you've found us now." And this was such an unexpectedly nice thing for him to say that Freya was caught off guard when he said, "Ready?" and pulled back the lid.

Moriarty shot out and up, a jagged piece of very-dark against the darkness, unfurling from something small and ugly into something majestic. He rose with astonishing speed and was gone, away from Throgmorton's, off into the city beyond.

"Goodbye," whispered Freya. For all she knew, Moriarty might have ultrasonically replied. She liked to think he had. The three of them stood for a minute, watching the sky.

"Let's go back," said Daniel. "Dad will be done by now."

They squelched back. Freya noticed all over again how cold she was, and hurried as fast as the mulch and mud allowed. But just outside the door, Esmie stopped, and tugged Daniel's sleeve; he stopped at once, and looked at her.

"She should come tonight," said Esmie.

The twins blinked at each other, two matching pairs of wide eyes over two upturned collars.

"Is that safe?" said Daniel. He considered Freya. "She might talk."

Esmie repeated obstinately, "She should come."

Daniel shrugged. "Fine." Then, to Freya, "We're going to the Society tonight to check that Moriarty got home safely," he said. "Want to come?"

Freya's heart leapt. "When?"

"Night-time. Once everyone's in bed. Are you in?"

Before Freya could reply, Esmie whispered, "Meet you at the Society. At midnight!" Then she and Daniel hurried inside, leaving Freya to follow in their wake. They pattered back through the twisting hallways as though they had known them all their lives.

Inside, Mr Stone and Miss Henderson were saying their goodbyes.

"Ah," said Mr Stone, spotting Daniel. "Is the bat safely in the car?"

"Yep," said Daniel. "All safe." He looked absolutely innocent. Freya was impressed.

"Excellent. Well, we'd best be going. A pleasure, Miss Henderson."

Miss Henderson bowed her head graciously. The twins followed their father out without a word, but as they left, Esmie nodded at Freya. Freya nodded back, very slightly; but she wasn't sure whether she was nodding yes or nodding goodbye.

She made her way slowly back across the entrance hall – past Miss Richards, who was studying the Dragon with fascination, comparing the runes to a battered old book; past a gaggle of girls admiring

Abigail's newly bandaged ankle, who stopped to glare at her as she walked past; up the central staircase and, entirely lost in thought, almost right into Miss Featherly.

"Ah, Freya! Our little troublemaker!" Miss Featherly said. She was putting some binoculars into a beautiful leather handbag and looking especially dreamy. "How are you, my dear? Not too upset by your encounter with *chiroptera*, I hope?"

"That means bats, Freya," supplied Henny, coming up the stairs behind her. "Latin name – *chiroptera*."

Freya did actually know this, as she had learned Latin from her dad, but it seemed rude to say so.

"Tonight," Miss Featherly announced, "I am going bat-watching! *So* inspiring. Wings like bits of umbrella – quite so!"

"I *think* bats will be hibernating right now," said Henny helpfully.

Miss Featherly drew herself up with

great dignity. "Miss Henderson," she said, "I think perhaps you do not appreciate the true meaning of Great Literature."

"Probably," agreed Henny cheerfully. "I don't understand a lot of it. I *am* reading a jolly good book though – you might like it. It's about a woman called Millicent Leatherby, terribly exciting, she's a space-cowgirl-detective from the year three thousand. . ."

Freya wondered whether she would remain trapped between the two teachers all night. Happily, the English mistress did not seem to think that Millicent Leatherby the space-cowgirl-detective was worth discussing. She glared at Henny, then swept down the stairs and on to the front door.

Freya looked at Henny and shrugged. The front door shut with a dignified thud.

"Oh dear," said Henny. "She really won't see any bats, I'm afraid. Oh, what a shame."

Freya agreed that this was indeed a shame. Happily, the headmistress emerged from her study just then to summon Henny, who went tottering back down the stairs again, looking as nervous as she always did around her sister. So Freya was at last free to fly up the stairs and along the winding corridors, through the lace of lamplight and shadow, back to her room.

She curled up on her window seat, hugging her knees, and pressed her head against the windowpane. Below her, the tops of the school's trees reached upwards, straining away from Throgmorton's, up towards the sky.

Miss Featherly would not see bats tonight. But Freya could, if she wanted to. And she really, really did want to. Very much.

The trouble was, it was probably a monumentally bad idea.

After everyone else had gone to bed, Freya sat on her window seat in the dark, jangling her keys. We'll talk about her in a moment. For now, I want to draw your attention to the moth on her ceiling.

He was going wild.

This was because, unlike humans, moths can hear bats. And when they hear a bat echolocating, they have to act sharpish if they don't want to end up on the wrong side of the bat – which is to say, the inside.

Unfortunately, moths are a bit dim, and easily muddled. For a start, they are confused by bright lights, and fly straight at them – no one knows why for sure, but they are very enthusiastic about it, and do it over and over again, even when it hurts. And they can't tell the difference between the clattering calls of a hungry bat and, say, a jangling bunch of keys.

The world must seem very alarming to a moth.

The Throgmorton Society for Science, Invention and Exploration

Freya could not decide.

She jangled the keys. With each jangle, she changed her mind.

Jangle. She would stay. She could probably be expelled for leaving the school at night, and her dad would be so disappointed in her. She had promised him that she would make the most of school.

Jangle. She would go. She wanted to see her bat

again. And the twins. And she badly wanted to get out of Throgmorton's, even just for one night.

Jangle. She would stay.

Jangle. She would go.

Freya's father had shown her once how keys worked – how each lock contains a row of metal pins and springs, and only the right key with the right prongs and ridges will push all the pins to line up perfectly and open the door.

Dr Robinson was the sort of person who knew everything. Once Freya had asked him how he knew so much, and he said that whenever he was worrying, he would learn about something that was bigger and more interesting than his worry. He had learned about all sorts of things that way.

"Does it make you feel better?" Freya had asked.

"Not *always*," he said. "But often."

"What if you run out of new things to learn?"

"That will never happen, Freya." He had smiled at her. "Not if you keep looking under the surface of things. The world is much more magical and mysterious than you think it is."

That last bit was quite hard to believe at

Throgmorton's, where bells and uniforms and rules and not-asking-any-questions made everything about as unmagical and unmysterious as it could possibly be. But Freya *tried* to believe it.

Her dad would be visiting in just four days' time, when he came for the party in his honour, and Freya didn't want to ruin that by getting into serious trouble and letting him down. That made up her mind. She put down the keys, changed into her grey-and-black striped pyjamas, and got into bed. It was chilly, and she pulled the covers tight.

As she shut her eyes, there was a whisper outside her room, and a giggle; then there was a rustle, and a slip of white paper appeared under the door.

Freya opened her eyes, and sat up.

She got back out of bed, went to the door, and picked up the note. It had been folded in half and half and half again, and it was thick with writing on both sides. When at last it was unfolded, she read:

Freya Robinson,
    We the undersigned are writing to inform you that no one will be speaking to you until Abigail's

ankle has fully healed. We hope you will think about what you have done.

The rest of the paper was covered in names.

Freya read each name one by one, until she was sure that every girl in her class was there. Even Quiet Carol, in apologetically tiny writing. Then she dropped the note on the floor.

She put on her blazer and stuffed her coat and shoes into her satchel. She put a pillow under the blankets, to give them a bulky look in the darkness. Then she crept out of her room.

Throgmorton's was cold at night. It seeped right into you, like a spell urging you to stay in bed where it was warm.

The spell wouldn't work on Freya. Not tonight.

She crept round and round the twisting hallways, past the tapestries and statues and dozens of Lord Throgmortons. (One of the portraits had been painted over, badly, where the bucket had hit it; presumably Mrs Clod's work.)

She crept, *extra* softly, down the spiralling staircase

where each mistress had a study. This was a great tall staircase wrapped around an enormous central stone pillar. Sound was magnified hugely here; it was known as the snitching staircase, because it was so hard to sneak past the mistresses undetected. Even creeping, Freya's footsteps were audible.

Only Henny's study showed a light. Everyone knew she was up every night working on her scientific ideas; one famous time she had been so engrossed that she had missed a fire alarm going off. And the fire was in her own bin. So Henny was not really a threat; but still, Freya held her breath. She wondered, as she crept past, whether the science mistress was still working on her theories about the Dragons' curse.

She survived the snitching staircase, hurried through the winding hallways, and crept down the steps to the entrance hall. The ivory Dragon watched her descend.

At the bottom, all was still. She was grateful that Miss Henderson had left for her conference: the headmistress's study was dark.

Then a door on her left opened, sending her diving behind a grandfather clock.

She was sure her heartbeat must be loud enough to hear, but the figure who hurried past did not turn her way. It was Miss Richards. The history teacher tip-tapped over to the Dragon statuette. She stooped and clicked on a torch. Freya could just make out her book of runes in one hand.

The torch darted back and forth between Dragon and book. Miss Richards let out a faint gasp. It seemed she'd had some sort of night-time epiphany.

Freya hoped it would be a quick epiphany. But it didn't seem to be. The minutes ticked by, and still Miss Richards stood there in rapt fascination, staring from book to Dragon, Dragon to book.

Freya realized she was going to have to take drastic action if she didn't want to miss the twins. Miss Richards seemed thoroughly absorbed; it was worth taking the chance. As quietly as she could, she scurried out from behind the clock and darted into a corridor beyond.

She thought she heard the history mistress shifting behind her, and her heart somersaulted. But there was no voice calling after her – no footsteps – no pursuit. Freya had made it.

There was no time for relief. She was running late now. She hurried past more paintings of His Lordship, and the school office, and the art rooms, and the patched-up lab Henny had famously blown up. At last she reached the back door, and wrenched it open.

Rain hammered down, roaring at her to stay inside.

She stepped outside.

The trees waved their branches frantically, urging her to go back in again.

She squelched resolutely forward.

WARNING, said the sign on the back gate, LEAVING THE GROUNDS WITHOUT PERMISSION WILL RESULT IN IMMEDIATE EXPULSION AND DISGRACE.

The bolts on the gate were stiff. But at last, with a squeal of protest, they gave way.

Then Freya was outside and running furiously through the rain. It felt wonderful to be out of the school, and to run, which was against several school rules unless you were holding a lacrosse stick.

At the Society, she slowed.

The Throgmorton Society for Science, Invention and Exploration was a red-brick fortress, with a square tower at each corner. One of the towers had a clock. It was four minutes past midnight: she was late. And there was no sign of the twins.

Maybe they just weren't here yet. Freya was suddenly very aware how wet her socks were. When she was nervous, she shifted from foot to foot, and now her socks made an uncomfortable *squitchett* with every shift.

Maybe they weren't coming.

Then a voice overhead said "Hello!", and Freya looked up. The twins hung from two street lights, one on either side of her.

Freya grinned up and waved, and the twins

shimmied down to join her. They were each wrapped in their great black coats and enormous red scarves, with their glasses peeping out above.

"We thought you weren't coming!" said Daniel.

"So did I, nearly," said Freya. "But I changed my mind. Where's Moriarty's roost?"

Daniel pointed up at one of the four turrets of the Society. "Up there. Ever been in the Society before?"

"Nope," said Freya. She had met Society people at Trust parties with her dad, once or twice, but she had never been inside the Society itself. The men and women who worked at the Society were known as Fellows, and the Trust paid them to think up scientific theories and invent things and do experiments. It was a very prestigious job, and you had to submit a good enough invention or paper to be invited to join. Poor Henny, of course, had had no luck – presumably because of the way her more interesting ideas tended to blow up or catch fire.

"It's brilliant in there," said Daniel. "Follow us. There's a side door which is bolted from the inside and there's a crack at the top. If I stand on top of Esmie and use this wire hook we've made, we can get it open." He held out a twisted bit of metal. "That leads us into the Baffington Wing, then on through the Higgs-Harriot Hall and out into the Morley Quad which leads to the old observatory tower, which is boarded up, but a plank in one of the windows is loose. That's how we get into the roost. OK?"

"No idea what you just said," said Freya, who had got lost somewhere around "Baffington". "I'll just follow."

"Great."

They hurried round the side, and Esmie produced a piece of wire. The twins stacked themselves one on top of the other and set to work. It occurred to Freya at this point that she had her father's keys, which would make life easier; but it seemed a bit late to say that now.

The door was old and peeling, with the words *Audi sonum cosmi* carved above it, beneath a stone owl – the Society's emblem. Freya squinted at the Latin. *Audi*: listen. *Sonum*, from *sono*, to make a sound. It said *Listen to the sound of the universe*.

Freya thought her dad would approve of that.

There was a scrape and sigh from the door, and it

eased open. On the other side hung a heavy curtain, thick with dust. Clearly, no one came through this door these days. Except the twins – and, tonight, Freya.

Inside, the first thing to hit Freya was the warmth. It was a welcoming warmth: the sort you find at firesides and under blankets.

Then her eyes began to adjust, and in the gloom she could make out the shadows of plush armchairs, the walls filled with books, the empty fireplaces. The carpet under her feet was thick and soft. The Society seemed to be waiting for them.

A door on the left was ajar, and Freya could dimly see a laboratory, which she itched to explore. But the twins were already hurrying on ahead to the next room, so she followed. This was a long gallery, and great instruments stood on plinths along its length – except the plinth at the far end, which held one of the Dragons.

GYROPROCTOR, read the plaque under what looked like a great golden sycamore seed. A long silvery tube in a velvet case was apparently a THERMOSTRATIOGRAPHIC. The brass binoculars with cogs and dials all over were called SONOSCOPES.

Freya breathed the names to herself. What did they all do?

The twins had already left the room behind. Freya followed, with one last long look at the strange hallway.

She stepped out into the courtyard beyond. At the far side, the twins were easing a plank out of the boarded-up turret in the corner.

"We'll go in first, then help you in, OK?" said Daniel. And they began shimmying through the window. They dropped down inside, and Freya followed.

"This is the old observatory tower," whispered Daniel. "They decided the structure wasn't safe and sealed it off years ago. It's perfect for the bats. There's an old telescope. D'you like telescopes? D'you know much about space?"

"Shh," suggested Esmie.

The three of them climbed the old stone steps in silence. Freya concentrated on the two-headed shadow ahead of her, trying not to wonder why the tower had been deemed unsafe.

She forgot all about structural safety when they

reached the small room at the very top of the tower. As Daniel had promised, there was an enormous telescope, waiting on wheels in the centre of the room. On all four sides there were open windows, now overhung with ivy. The ceiling was painted with constellations (and Lord Throgmorton's face), and everything was covered in a dusting of cobwebs.

"Wow," said Freya.

Esmie produced a torch and set it at the foot of the telescope, so that only the softest light disturbed the ceiling. It was just enough to show them the huddle of bats that hung upside down in the corner, clinging to each other, furry bodies wrapped up tightly in their wings.

"There they are," whispered Daniel. "And Moriarty's safe. That's him." Freya peered through the gloom at the bat Daniel pointed out. *Her* bat. He looked snug.

"That's good news, then," she said. "He made it home."

"Very good news," said Daniel. He showed Freya the notebook, which contained a map showing the seven Throgmorton buildings in the city. All were marked

with a bat and a number. "Each bat shows where there's a roost – this year there's one in all the Throgmorton buildings. Your school has one in an old turret – we decided not to mention that to your headmistress."

"And the ticks?" said Freya, pointing to the ticks that had been inked next to the roosts.

"Means they're all home safely," he said. "The thing is, Freya, your bat wasn't the first to wake up. Bats have been waking from all the roosts this week, a new one every day. It's so weird. Dad can't figure out why. It's winter – they ought to be sleeping. All seven roosts in one week!"

Freya examined the ticks. "So you checked up on all the other roosts before tonight?" she said.

"Yep," said Daniel.

"Except for Nimrod," objected Esmie.

"Oh yeah," said Daniel. "Nimrod lives alone in the museum, and we can't get in there."

The twins sat down at the foot of the telescope, faces uplit by the torch. Freya joined them. For a moment no one spoke, except the wind whispering through the ivy.

"Are you worried about Nimrod?" said Freya.

"Yes," said Esmie, and at the same time, Daniel said, "Yep, but there's nothing we can do about it. The museum is locked." Esmie looked like she might say more, but Daniel was charging on. "Do you like it up here, Freya? It's one of my favourite roosts. My *favourite* favourite is the church bell tower. Have you ever been in there?"

"No." Freya hugged her knees for warmth. "How do you get in to all these places?"

"Oh, there's a different knack for all of them. You saw the side door here. The theatre has an old window in the ladies' loos that doesn't lock. The church has a tunnel into the crypt, it's a bit creepy. . ."

"Daniel," said Esmie. "Quiet a minute. Show Freya what we brought."

"Oh!" said Daniel. "Yes!" He fumbled in his coat pocket, and produced a tin. Four eyes blinked at Freya expectantly.

"Um," she said.

"Condensed milk!" said Daniel. "You said you wanted to try it. We found some in the cupboard at home."

"Midnight feast," explained Esmie, bringing out a tin opener.

"Oh!" said Freya. And this was so nice, she said "Oh!" again for good measure. She took the tin and the tin opener and took off the lid. Inside was something thick and white and goopy. "Honestly, I don't really know what it is," she said. "I guess we should just stick our fingers in. . .?"

So they did. The condensed milk was very sweet, and quite nice, although if the girls in the boarding school books were really eating so much of it they must have felt very sick. Freya wouldn't have cared if it had tasted of vinegar. She was having a midnight feast at last, at the top of a tower amid whispering ivy, with two of the strangest and most unexpected friends she had ever had.

"Mmm," said Daniel. "It's pretty tasty. Is this how you imagined it?"

Freya laughed. "Not even a little bit. It's better." She licked her lips, savouring the sweetness. "Thank you. So much. For inviting me, I mean, and for the milk. I wish I could do something for you."

She hugged her knees to her chest, feeling the reassuring bulk of the keys in her blazer pocket. And that's when she realized that she *could* do something for the twins, after all.

It wasn't a very sensible idea. It was a lot more serious than just breaking school rules. But she pushed her doubts away. There would be time for worrying later.

"I've just realized – I've got my dad's key for the museum. I can get you inside!"

In the grounds of the museum, a fox knew that the children passed by, although the children never knew about the fox.

Foxes hear astonishingly well. That night was a symphony for the fox: his ears spun to catch every rustling leaf, every skittering paw, every scurrying creature underground.

He heard the three great galumphing children before they even got close. With a flick of his tail, he turned away, and trotted off into the night.

The Throgmorton Museum

Freya didn't regret her decision until they were inside the museum. Unfortunately, inside was very much the wrong side for regrets.

She had seen the museum plenty of times in daylight, but it was a different place at night. It was cavernous, and full of echoes and shadows that didn't seem to belong to anything. And it was cold.

For a moment, they all stood huddled in the entrance hall, next to the statue of Lord Throgmorton with arms thrown wide in welcome.

"I've never been here in the dark," whispered Daniel.

His voice fluttered pathetically in the enormous air. "Bit creepy, isn't it?"

The others didn't reply. Three mummies stood upright in sarcophagi, looking at them all. They were not exactly encouraging.

But for Freya, the real problem was not the dark or the cold or the mummies. The moment she had stepped into the museum's secretive, quiet smell, so familiar to her, memories of her dad had come rushing back. She suddenly realized how appalled he would be if he knew she was breaking in to his beloved museum. She didn't mind breaking stupid school rules, but this was different: her dad trusted her. And she was using his keys to trespass. He had wanted them kept safe – handed in – not used for night-time break-ins.

It had seemed like such a good idea when they were whispering together amidst the ivy. That had been an unreal, adventure place. But now it was real.

The mummies weren't helping.

But it was too late for regrets. The twins were already trotting off past the discouraging mummies and up the wide stone steps, which led to an even more discouraging skeleton of a Tyrannosaurus rex. Halfway up, Esmie turned and looked back.

"Coming?" she asked.

Freya wanted to say that they should all turn back. But Daniel was still climbing the steps as fast as his short legs would carry him, and she had a feeling that whatever she said, the twins would not be leaving here until they had checked on Nimrod. So she nodded – she didn't like to speak in that enormous silence – and hurried up the steps behind them.

The twins seemed to know exactly where they were going. They led Freya through a hall of statues with limbs missing, and another full of severe six-foot vases, to a corkscrew staircase which wound up and up and up, getting dustier and more abandoned with every turn. Even Daniel didn't speak. They all felt the weight of the museum's silence.

The staircase led to a creaky storeroom at the top of the building, where the shapes of unknown old-and-odd things bulged under dust sheets. Esmie walked to a spot on the far left, laid down the torch, turned it on and looked up.

There was nothing there.

Daniel climbed on something dust-sheeted-and-probably-priceless to get a better look.

"Be careful," said Freya.

"Don't worry," said Daniel. "I'm a really good climber." Which was obvious, but the real question was whether the probably-priceless things were good at being climbed on. Freya held her breath, waiting for some precious artefact to crack or smash or crumble.

But nothing did. Daniel shimmied around the room, clambering over the dustsheets as though they were a playground obstacle course, Esmie holding the torch. When they had done a circuit of the whole room, he scrambled down, and they all looked at each other in the torchlight.

"Nimrod isn't here," Esmie concluded. She got out her notebook and made a mark next to the museum.

"Maybe he's still out hunting," said Daniel. "Don't worry, Esmie."

They were all silent for a moment.

"Shall we go?" said Freya at last. The sooner they

were out of here, she thought, the sooner she could pretend she had never broken in.

"Straight away?" said Daniel. "Don't you want to look around?"

"I've seen it," Freya said quickly.

"That's in the day, full of other people. It's different in the dark. Don't you think?"

If by "different" Daniel meant "very, very creepy", then Freya agreed. But he was already trotting off down the stairs.

Freya realized then that Daniel was the sort of person who was fun to be around when you liked his ideas, and not so much fun when you didn't. Some people are like that: they keep flowing along like a river, and trying to swim against the current is exhausting.

She followed Daniel as he trotted eagerly through fossils and weapons and broken pottery. Throughout, she kept up a steady stream of reasons why they should leave. When they reached the Special Eldrida Exhibit Room, Esmie stopped, and held up a hand.

"Freya's not happy," she said. "We should go."

"Aren't you?" said Daniel to Freya, surprised. "But this is the good bit. Come on!"

Esmie stood her ground.

"You look if you want," she said. "I'm taking Freya outside."

"OK," said Daniel. He shrugged. Then he set off into the next room, a tiny figure swallowed up by the dark archway.

Esmie and Freya walked back to the wide stone steps, past the dinosaur and the discouraging mummies, out on to the lawns of the museum. The rain had eased to a heavy drizzle. They huddled under a tree.

"Thanks," said Freya, taking a deep breath. "I was getting a bit panicky in there. Breaking in, you know. It's my dad's key, and he trusted me. . ."

Esmie nodded. Freya had assumed she was quiet to make room for Daniel, but she didn't say anything now either. She watched as Esmie climbed on to the lower branch of the tree and hung there by her knees, swaying gently.

"Why do you hang upside down so much?" Freya asked.

"It's interesting," said Esmie, her voice muffled by her scarf. "You see things differently."

After a minute, Freya climbed up after her to try it out. Blood rushed to her head, which made her a bit dizzy, but it felt friendly, hanging there together.

Perhaps, if she had been the right way up, the next few minutes wouldn't have been such a muddle in her head afterwards.

Daniel came shooting out of the museum at an astonishing speed, coat billowing. He was carrying a bucket, holding it out carefully ahead of him.

Esmie dropped down neatly, but it took Freya longer. By the time she was on the ground, Daniel had reached the tree.

"Someone's in there," he said. "Think they saw me. Let's go."

Without another word, the three of them set off across the lawn at full pelt. Freya felt sick. Who was it that Daniel had seen in there? Museum security?

"Daniel," she panted. "What's in the bucket?"

"Nimrod," wheezed Daniel. "Found him in the exhibit room. Borrowed bucket from a cleaning cupboard. He's injured. We'll need to take him to Dad."

"Is it bad?" said Esmie.

"One wing," said Daniel.

After that they ran in silence, until they were well clear of the museum. At a fork in the road beyond, the twins stopped suddenly, and Freya stumbled to a halt behind them.

"We – go – this – way," explained Daniel. He gulped an enormous breath. "We'll be in touch soon, OK?" And bucket aloft, he and Esmie trotted off, leaving Freya to head back through the rain to school.

She ran all the way, as though running would somehow help. It felt as though the last hour was a bad dream that she could unravel if she ran fast enough.

And it wasn't over yet. She was halfway across the school gardens when she heard a steady stream of muttering coming from the bins. This was mysterious, until one of the shadow bins straightened up and she realized it was in fact Mrs Clod, rummaging through the rubbish. Which was still quite mysterious, and a nuisance.

Freya hid in a rain-soaked bush and waited five freezing minutes for Mrs Clod to finish whatever she was doing in the bins. She had not bargained on the school being so lively at night. First Henny in her study, then Miss Richards in the entrance hall, and now Mrs Clod. It was maddening.

She tried very hard to think about something more magical and mysterious than her sodden state, as her dad would recommend. She squinted up at the stars through the rain and practised naming them in her head, and thinking about how even the very closest one is over four light years away and they are all rushing outwards all the time as the universe expands and some of them are already dead. This half worked, but her legs ached, and she was shivering.

At last Mrs Clod stopped rummaging and went inside. Freya waited a minute, then *squitchett*ed across the mulch, took out her dad's keys, and let herself in.

She wiped her shoes and wrung out her hair as best she could to avoid leaving a trail, then crept back through the hallways, past the now-dark studies of the snitching staircase, past a dozen Throgmortons-and-cats, back to the best room in the school which had caused her so much unhappiness.

Safely inside, she took off her soaked pyjamas, put on her uniform for warmth, got into her bed, and dropped into sleep like a stone into water.

While Freya slept, dawn came, and a woodpigeon woke in the school grounds and pushed off into the sky. She had come from Norway, and she was on her way to spend the winter in warm Spanish oak woods.

The woodpigeon didn't need a map, because she was following the tug of a magnet.

This wasn't one of those little magnets you use to stick things on the fridge. It was the planet: the Earth itself is one giant magnet, thanks to the molten metal at its heart. A woodpigeon can feel this magnet tugging at it, and from that, it knows which way is north, and can fly wherever it wants to go.

This is brilliant and astonishing and extraordinary. It also means that if you put a big magnet next to a pigeon, it gets very confused.

Freya could feel the pull of elsewhere too – of her own home, which wasn't a fixed place, but always with her dad. She couldn't fly there, of course. Being able to fly is not a human thing. But it is probably very human to wish that you could, sometimes.

The vanishing Eldrida Dragons

The next morning, Freya woke late.

She had been dreaming. She had been up in the observatory tower, and all the bats were awake and flying overhead, and Daniel was flying around too, asking them all why they had woken up. But the bats just laughed at him and flapped away. Then Esmie was there, asking Freya why she *wasn't* waking up – and then the observatory tower melted away, and Freya was in her own bed, awake.

For one brief moment, she felt completely peaceful.

Then she realized it was light outside.

This was strange. She should have been woken in the dark by the school bell. Had she missed it?

She had a bad feeling about this.

She got out of bed, reached for her uniform, and realized she was already wearing it. Then she remembered why.

She went out into the hallway. To her left and right, there was cosy giggling and murmuring in the other girls' rooms. Why weren't they in class? Freya glanced at her watch. She should have been in the chalk-dust stupor of a geography lesson by now. There was no one to ask, except for Lord Throgmorton over the doorway, looking at her through a painted magnifying glass.

"Well?" she asked him. "What's going on?"

His half-amused smile gave nothing away.

Then, as though summoned by His Lordship, Abigail and Zara appeared through the doorway under his portrait, arm in arm. They might know. Of course, officially they weren't speaking to Freya. But on the other hand, they did both *love* announcing things.

"What's going on?" Freya asked.

They ignored her, striding past, their feet and ponytails in perfect unison.

Freya looked at Lord Throgmorton and shrugged.

But just before they went into Zara's room, Abigail shot over her shoulder: *"You'll* know what's going on soon enough, Freya Robinson."

This did not sound good.

Freya made her way downstairs. She passed no one in the spiderweb hallways. The curtains in the assembly hall were still closed; the dining hall chairs were still placed upside down on the tables.

The entrance hall was empty. Through the windows, Freya could see that the driveway was very much not empty. More precisely, it contained a car. Even more precisely, it contained a *police* car.

She told herself firmly that there was no reason to think that the police car had anything to do with last night, and she tried to think about something bigger and more interesting, while she felt for the comforting weight of the keys in her blazer pocket. But then she felt a wave of hot and cold, both at once, from her head down to her toes, as she realized something terrible.

The keys weren't there.

She must have dropped them – but where? This was exactly why her dad had wanted her to hand them in. Freya felt an urgent need to sit down, but before she had time to connect her brain to her legs, the door of Miss Henderson's office opened and Henny came out.

"Oh d-dear, Freya," she said, when she saw her – and from the quiver of her cardigan, Freya thought it was even more *oh dear* than usual.

"What's going on, miss? Why aren't we in class?"

"Well – there's been a spot of – you see – oh *dear*," explained Henny. She attempted a comforting smile. "Still, not to worry."

From Miss Henderson's study, the headmistress called, "Is that *her* out there, Clarissa?"

"Y-yes. . ."

"Well don't stand there dithering. Send her in."

Henny nodded three times and gave Freya a reassuring squeeze on the shoulder, before hurrying off in the least reassuring way possible.

Freya gathered all her courage, went to the study, and knocked.

Miss Henderson was at her desk. There were also two police officers. The first had tawny hair and a hawk-like face, and she looked at Freya with sharp interest. The second looked more like an owl than a hawk, with a heart-shaped face and big round eyes, and he was very busy doodling flowers in his notebook. Miss Henderson had served fancy chocolates on little silver dishes, but nobody was eating them.

"Hello," said Freya.

"Hello," said the owl-officer. The hawk-officer said nothing.

"Freya," said Miss Henderson, "I have been summoned back to my school from my little hotel in Sodden-Under-Foot at the crack of dawn. I am missing my conference. Can you possibly imagine why, child?"

Freya tried to look like somebody who couldn't. And in fact, she couldn't *exactly*. She just had a horrible feeling that last night, and the missing keys, came into it all somehow.

"This," Miss Henderson went on, "is DI North" – a nod from the hawk – "and PC Fig" – a wave from the owl, who dropped his pen, then dropped his notebook trying to pick up the pen, then recovered the notebook, then smiled at everyone.

Miss Henderson contemplated him sternly, licked her lips, and turned back to Freya. "DI North," she explained, "would like to ask you some questions. She can be an uncooperative child, Detective, but if there is any trouble—"

DI North cut her off with the kind of "Thank you" that means "Stop talking". Then she leaned forward.

"Freya Robinson?"

"Yes," said Freya. The detective's voice was kinder than she had expected.

"Last night, Freya, seven very valuable Dragon statues were stolen from each of the seven Throgmorton buildings, including this school. We were alerted by the church first, as they had an early morning service, and we immediately inspected all seven sites. None of the buildings show any sign of forced entry. Your father's keys were found outside the museum, under a tree. Keys, it seems, to all seven buildings." Saying this, DI North produced Dr Robinson's keys and put them on Miss Henderson's desk.

Freya remembered hanging upside down, giddy with the blood rushing to her head.

"We have been told," DI North went on, "that you carry these keys at all times. How do you think they come to be under that tree, Freya?"

"I don't know. I lost them." Freya would not have described herself as a natural liar, but she found it came easily enough, when circumstances were desperate.

DI North nodded. "When did you last have them?"

"After dinner, but before bed."

"I see. Did you leave the school last night?"

"No – ooo."

Halfway through her "no" Freya realized that this created all sorts of problems. If she claimed to have lost the keys in the school, then only someone in the school could have found and used them. But it was too late to change her mind now, and besides, she couldn't think of a harmless night-time jaunt fast enough.

"Are you sure, Freya?" DI North leaned forward. "It's very important. We have to assume the keys were used by the thief, you see – very lucky for us that they dropped them. Without any obvious sign of a break-in, it's our best explanation at the moment."

Freya thought, but didn't say, that *she* had another explanation. She knew two people who had worked out how to wriggle into all of those buildings without leaving a trace – or at least, all except the museum.

And she had helped them with that. She had let them both into the museum, left Daniel alone in the special exhibition, and run away with him, as he carefully carried something hidden in a bucket. Nimrod, he had said. Or, as it turned out, *an Eldrida Dragon*.

Had she really believed the twins had invited her to join them last night just because they liked her? She had told them all about her dad's prize, and the keys. *That* was why Esmie had been so keen for her to join them. They were thieves.

DI North was still talking. "Miss Henderson, I'm afraid I'm going to have to speak with everyone on the school premises who had the opportunity to steal these keys. I will start, please, by taking statements on where everybody was last night, so I can get on with some basic fact-checking. Meanwhile I'll have officers at the front and back door to search anybody leaving, and we'll need to search outgoing post and bins – to ensure no evidence is removed."

Miss Henderson, who until now had been glaring icily at Freya, turned her bulging eyes to DI North, eyebrows surging upwards. The detective ignored this, and continued. "PC Fig will stay here to oversee the operation. Perhaps you could find him a room to sleep in?"

"Detective," said Miss Henderson, with a furious lick of her lips, "this is a *respectable* school. If anybody learns that my staff are under suspicion. . . That we are guarded by police! The effect on our reputation—"

"Miss Henderson," said DI North, "I understand your concern. But it is necessary."

From the way she spoke, there was clearly no use in any further argument. Miss Henderson had to settle for glaring at Freya some more instead, to relieve her feelings. Freya decided that if circumstances had been different, she might have quite liked the detective. But then again, judging by last night, she didn't have very good taste in people.

"One more thing, Freya," said DI North. "When we informed Lord Throgmorton, he was very keen that this be kept out of the press, and in particular did not want to call Dr Robinson yet. He, er, was quite insistent that the Dragons *will* be found, and soon. I gather there is a . . . party, and he wishes it to go ahead as planned." She looked carefully neutral. "While I can't control what you say to your own father, Freya, I have been asked to pass this on."

The Throgmorton Trust was run by the current, very elderly Lord Throgmorton, Lord Joseph Edward Throgmorton the Third – more commonly known as Throg Three. Freya had never met him, but her dad had once, at a fancy gala dinner. Apparently His Lordship had been served the wrong dessert, and had thrown the dessert in question at the waiter, along with the desserts of five other people, and the sugar bowl for good measure.

So Freya didn't particularly care what Throg Three wanted. But she also really, really didn't want to *ever* discuss this with her father. So she just nodded. From the way Miss Henderson tutted, it was obvious that *she* was itching to have the pleasure of calling him, and telling him about Freya's disastrous carelessness and the loss of his Dragons in one satisfying swoop. But Throg Three was not disobeyed lightly.

"Right. We may have more questions later," said DI North. "Please don't leave the school. Although I gather there's some sort of demerit system which means you aren't allowed on any outings at present anyway." A very slight tilt to the detective's eyebrows suggested that she neither knew nor cared what a demerit was. "Do you have any questions for us?" she said. "I realize this must be quite overwhelming."

"Do you have any theories yet?" asked Freya, wondering what else the detective knew – and how close she was to the awful truth.

DI North shook her head. "No suspects, no. No windows or locks were broken, so we're confident keys were used. And since Lord Throgmorton himself is the only other person with a complete set of keys, it was almost certainly these keys here. Now—"

"I have a theory!" announced PC Fig.

Detective North didn't exactly roll her eyes, but Freya was sure she had to stop herself. "PC Fig is following some leads, but—"

"I saw in the paper that there's been a strange spate of rogue bats waking up, all in Throgmorton's buildings," Fig explained, leaning forward excitedly. "Everyone knows that bats don't wake up in the winter. So – hear me out – my theory is that maybe the *bats* took the Dragons." He looked around at them all eagerly. Miss Henderson let out a faint snort. "Like how magpies take shiny things. There was this famous silver theft once that turned out to be a magpie. . ."

"Yes, well, we—" said DI North.

"They'd have to work as a team to carry them," went on PC Fig, "But they're quite smart, bats are. And—"

"Thank you, PC Fig," said DI North, in that "stop talking" way she had used earlier.

PC Fig blushed and fell silent. Freya felt quite sorry for him. Except that she would really rather no one started thinking about the bats. It was too close to the truth for comfort.

"If you remember anything else," said DI North, "please let me know. Or if you want to correct anything you've told me." She stared at Freya extra piercingly as she said that last bit, and Freya suddenly wondered whether she wasn't so good at lying after all. "That's all for now," DI North said. "You can go."

Miss Henderson cleared her throat peevishly, and said, "Yes, Freya, you can go" – but Freya had already stood, and it was too late for Miss Henderson to pretend that she was in charge here. To make up for it, she added, "Thirty demerits for recklessly leaving those keys lying around. One more toe out of line, Freya, and I *will* call your father, whatever Lord Throgmorton might feel about it."

Freya fled from the study and hurried straight up to the attic, needing to be alone to think. What had she *done*? And who would ever believe that she had done it by mistake?

The attic door opened with a sigh. There was some part of Freya that hoped she would find the bat here again; that by coming back up here, she could start everything over and choose differently. But there was no bat today, just piles of forgotten junk and a lot of dust.

She stood very still for ten seconds, half expecting a flutter of wings – or maybe an upside-down boy, asking her if she was all right.

Neither of those things appeared. Freya Robinson sat down alone among the pipes and pendulums and periscopes. Then she put her head in her hands, and she cried.

That morning, a sparrowhawk hovered over the grounds of Throgmorton's School for Girls. He was waiting to kill.

He looked very majestic, his wide wings carving a dark slash into the grey sky; but the truth was, he spent most of the day looking at old, dried wee.

This isn't very glamorous, but it is quite clever, because when the sparrowhawk looks at that wee he is seeing something called ultraviolet light.

We need light to see anything at all. Light waves are sent out by the sun or a light bulb or whatever, and those waves bounce off objects and into our eyes. Every object bounces some kinds of light and not others, and that gives us different colours – for example, a really ripe tomato will only bounce red light, so it looks red and we know it's delicious and ready to eat.

Human eyes can see red, blue and green light, but we can't see a fourth kind of light called ultraviolet. Sparrowhawks can, and old dried wee bounces ultraviolet light brilliantly. So when little mice and voles leave trails of wee around, the *sparrowhawk sees a colourful map, pointing right to their dinner.*

It isn't glamorous. But it is deadly.

The forbidden cupboard
of Mrs Clod

It was Abigail, in her role as head girl, who sat down with the rule book and a sheet of paper to calculate which combination of punishments Freya would now be given. Even for Freya, it was a record number of demerits in one week.

Of course, Abigail couldn't actually speak to her about it: so at dinner, while Freya was eating her bland-lukewarm-not-quite-enough bowlful of leek soup, she marched over and put the list down while staring pointedly into the middle distance. She was so busy with the staring that she missed and put it in Quiet

Carol's soup. Then she marched off again, ponytail swaying at full mast.

Freya sponged the page dry with the tablecloth and examined it. Even in Abigail's neat, cramped handwriting, it was a long list of punishments.

It began at seven o'clock the next morning – which was a Saturday – for a full day of cleaning with Mrs Clod. Freya sighed. On the plus side, this meant she would miss assembly, and whatever poem Miss Featherly was planning to inflict on them. On the down side, it also meant missing breakfast.

So when the bell went the next morning, she dressed and went down to the entrance hall to meet Mrs Clod, joining the stream of girls flowing down to the assembly hall. No one was talking to her, of course, but all around her the rumours flew:

"It was Freya Robinson! Didn't you hear? They found her keys!"

"I reckon Miss Richards took them, she's obsessed with those Dragons."

"No, the bats did it – shut up, they *did* – that police officer was telling me so just this morning."

"It was *obviously* Freya. Her dad was probably in on it. . ."

Girls that passed near her suddenly fell quiet, so that in all the river of gossip, there was an eddy of silence around Freya Robinson.

As they all went on into assembly, Freya was left alone in the entrance hall – apart from PC Fig, who was now perched on a stool near the door, doodling in his notebook.

"Good morning, Freya!" he called – then, as the front door opened, "Ah, good morning, Mrs Clod."

The day outside was thick with fog, and Mrs Clod emerged from it in black wellies. She must have passed the postman on her way, because she had the day's post tucked under one arm.

"Morning, PC Fig. Got any proof it was the bats yet?" she asked cheerfully.

"Not yet," he said. He lowered his voice, presumably lest any bats should overhear. "But I'm working on it. I've been talking to a man at the conservation trust. Going to search the roosts on Monday, when I'm off duty here."

"You're off your rocker," said Mrs Clod; then she added knowingly, "Those Dragons are cursed, you know. This was always going to end badly." She turned to Freya. "Come on, then. Time to clean."

Freya waved goodbye to PC Fig and followed Mrs Clod, who was already heading away at full stomp, wellies smacking on the stone.

They stopped at the office first, for Mrs Clod to hand in the post; then stomped all the way to the snitching staircase, which echoed her stomps magnificently. Halfway up, she stopped by a lock-studded door. "This is my cupboard," she announced. "I keep it shut. You need anything, you ask me." She looked menacingly at Freya, hands on hips, eyes narrowed.

"OK," said Freya.

"And" – Mrs Clod reached into her bag and held out an envelope – "this came for you."

Freya took it. She recognized the neat black handwriting, and her breath caught.

Esmie.

"Thank you," she said.

As Mrs Clod took an enormous bunch of keys from

her waist and got started on her cupboard's endless locks, Freya tore open the envelope, and read:

Freya,
You'll know by now that the Eldrida Dragons have gone missing. I hope you don't think it was us. It wasn't.

Nimrod is doing well. He will be realeased again this evening.

We want to talk to you. We'll meet you tonight at midnight.

D & E x

Freya read it a second time. She desperately wanted to believe them. But she had already been fooled once, and she had promised herself she wouldn't be so stupid again. She certainly shouldn't have another midnight meeting with them.

And meet them *where*, anyway?

Mrs Clod, who had disappeared into her cupboard, re-emerged. "Now, this here's silver polish. If I catch you polishing anything other than silver with it, I'll polish *you* with it. Understood?"

Freya was set to work polishing the school's lacrosse trophies, which was quite good for her state of mind – it was satisfying, scrubbing hard, and seeing the silver come to life. She sat cross-legged on a window seat at the bottom of the staircase, the fog pressing at the window, and she polished those trophies until they gleamed. When the other girls streamed past on the way to their Saturday clubs, and some of them whispered about her as they passed, she just concentrated extra hard, and didn't listen.

She couldn't get her mind any clearer though.

When the trophies were done, Mrs Clod nodded her satisfaction. She led Freya back to the cupboard and produced a bucket and a mop.

"Floors!" she announced. "We need everywhere shipshape before this nonsense party. You can start with the gym. You'll need a bottle of bleach, hang on. . ."

Just then, Miss Richards appeared breathlessly on the stairs below.

"Oh, Mrs Clod," she said. "Clarissa is having a little

difficulty with Science Club. They've just spilled some sort of chemical all over the carpet – it's dissolving rather rapidly – is there anything we can. . .?"

Mrs Clod rolled her eyes, seized a bottle of something marked DANGEROUS, CLOD ONLY from the cupboard, and stomped off to battle whatever remained of Henny's carpet. Miss Richards followed. Freya was left alone.

The first thing she did was reread her letter from Esmie. It left her no clearer about what to do. She put it back in her blazer pocket.

Mrs Clod still didn't return. Freya spent an idle minute sitting on the stairs, wondering how things were going with the caretaker's rescue mission. She was *very* grateful that Henny had been forbidden to touch the school's Dragon; it would probably have gone the same way as the carpet by now.

Then she remembered, with a sick feeling, that the Dragon was missing now anyway; so it didn't make much difference.

It seemed impossible to think about something bigger and more interesting than her worries at the moment. Freya badly needed something to get on with, to take her mind off things. She knew she wasn't supposed to go in the cupboard, but she *had* been told to mop the gym floor – surely she could help herself to the bleach.

The cupboard was much bigger than she had expected – more of a small room, really – and enormously cluttered. Clearly, Mrs Clod had a system all her own. Locating a bottle of bleach was not easy. There were lots of identical spray bottles, with labels like QUITE DANGEROUS, DO NOT DRINK and VERY DANGEROUS, DO NOT LOOK AT DIRECTLY. They were buried in amongst all sorts of cloths and dusters and hammers and spanners and wire wool and bags and buckets and one very alarming chainsaw. There was a machine for cutting all Mrs Clod's keys, a furnace of some sort, and what looked like a cement mixer. . .

Freya started at one end, and from top to bottom began pulling out bottles to read their labels.

Reaching for one high up on a shelf, she knocked a pile of papers, which cascaded unhelpfully all over the floor. She stooped to pick them up. There were lots of rather stained, torn old envelopes in the pile – and they were

addressed to Clarissa Henderson.

Why did Mrs Clod have letters for Henny in here?

The envelopes all had a sender label: THE SOCIETY FOR SCIENCE, INVENTION AND EXPLORATION. There was a little picture of an owl in blue ink. And a lot of the papers that had fallen out were, she saw, headed with the same owl.

Dear Clarissa Henderson,

read one,

Thank you for interesting proposal. Unfortunately, the high rate of combustion means we cannot accept the invention at present. However, we would be interested. . .

And another:

Dear Clarissa Henderson,

May I begin by offering my admiration for this complex and fascinating work. We will not be able to offer you a position here yet, as half the committee are unfortunately convinced that the whole paper is completely bananas. However, many of us thought. . .

And another:

Dear Clarissa,

Goodness, this one makes a loud bang! I regret. . .

And so on. The fruits of Henny's attempts to fulfil her dream and join the Society. Poor Henny. But why were her letters in Mrs Clod's cupboard?

A thud from somewhere in the distance brought Freya to her senses, and she began shuffling the papers back into a pile. She was just putting them back when she saw something on top that wasn't a letter.

She picked it up, curious. It was a pencil sketch, bound to several more with a paper clip. The first was headed M, and looked like this:

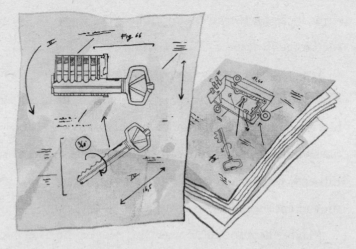

Freya stared. She had seen pictures like that before, the time that her dad had explained how locks worked. The picture was a cross-section of a lock, showing all the pins and springs. And below was the shape of the key that would match.

She thumbed through the next pages. SSIE, read one. T. SFB. C. L. SFG.

She translated in her head: M for Museum. SSIE, Society for Science, Invention and Exploration. Theatre. School for Boys. Church. Library. And on School for Girls, not one lock but three.

Each of the homes of the Eldrida Dragons – with

three locks for the girl's school, like the three locks on the Dragon's case.

Freya's heart raced. Had Mrs Clod *made* these keys? After all, her key-cutting machine was right here! Or had it been Henny? The sketches were with her letters – possibly they had fallen out of one of the envelopes. Either way, *somebody* besides Freya might have the keys they needed to take the Dragons.

Maybe the impossible was true. Maybe the thief had their own keys, and the twins really had just been in the wrong place at the wrong time.

Just then there were footsteps on the staircase. Freya shoved the papers back on the shelf hastily, grabbed a bottle at random to show in her defence, and scrambled out of the cupboard.

It wasn't Mrs Clod who appeared. It was Miss Featherly, clutching her ring-studded hands together and looking woeful. She always looked woeful on Saturdays, because it was clubs day, and nobody ever signed up for Poetry Club.

"Hello, Freya, dear," she said, with maximum woe on the word *dear*. "You weren't in assembly."

"No, miss. I'm cleaning today. Demerits."

"Such a shame," sighed Miss Featherly. "I had prepared a poem for you especially."

Of all the things that Freya thought were a shame about the situation, this was very low down the list. "Oh, no," she said, while wondering how she could persuade Miss Featherly to leave. She was kicking herself for panicking – she should have taken those sketches while she had the chance. She could have given them to DI North.

"It is one I penned myself," said Miss Featherly, "to try and capture what you must be feeling. It is called 'On a Morning Full of Crushing Guilt at the Consequences of My Carelessness.'" Her eyes lit up. "Perhaps," she said, "I could read it for you now?"

"Oh, thanks," said Freya. "But I need to – er" – she checked the bottle she had picked up: it said FOR TROPICAL PLANTS ONLY – "see to the . . . tropical plants. . ."

Miss Featherly looked confused, which was fair enough, since the school didn't have any tropical plants. "It will only take a moment," she said; and with a surprisingly strong grip, she steered Freya up the stairs and into her study.

Freya had a brief impression of glitzy ornaments and gilded furniture; there was even an unlikely antique chandelier on the ceiling. Then she was more or less pushed into an armchair, to gaze up at the English mistress.

"Now, you make yourself right at home, Freya." Miss Featherly smiled. "Close your eyes, and just breathe deeply."

"But Mrs Clod wants—"

She waved this aside. "I'm sure Mrs Clod will understand the need for poetry."

Freya was not at all sure this was true, but Miss Featherly had already unlocked a drawer of her desk, full of pages and pages covered in the pencilled loops and swirls of her handwriting. She stood over it protectively, as though Freya might peek. Then she produced the paper she wanted, and locked the drawer again with great care.

"Ahrrm," she said. She flung out one arm, and pronounced: "When filled with guilt, as slime fills up a pond—"

As she began, footsteps reverberated up the

snitching staircase, and Miss Richards stuck her head around the doorway.

"Lillian," she said, "I've just sent the Science Club over to your room. Can you supervise, maybe do some poetry with them? Mrs Clod is doing her best to limit the damage, but half of Felicity's shoe just dissolved and I don't think it's safe..."

"Of course," cried Miss Featherly, flushed pink with joy at the sudden revival of Poetry Club. "Freya, dear, why don't you take this to read later. Poor Felicity; I must think what might be comforting to read when one's shoe is dissolving..."

And Miss Featherly handed Freya her scribbled poem, and hurried to the door.

Freya breathed a sigh of relief: she could get the sketches back. But as she was walking to the door, Miss Richards stopped her. She looked very serious.

"Freya," she said, "could you pop into my study for a quick word?"

It was not really a question. Miss Richards could be *very* firm, sometimes. To Freya's intense frustration, instead of returning to Mrs Clod's cupboard, she found herself being shepherded up the next corkscrew turn of staircase to the history mistress's study.

She had never been in here, and at other times, she might have enjoyed it. The office felt homely to her. The walls were lined with books, and every spare inch of space was crowded with interesting replicas of statuettes and carvings and tapestries from ancient worlds. Here, Freya thought, was where Miss Richards's tidied-away sensibleness might relax.

But right now, she was still looking serious.

"Freya," she said, "I'm glad I got a chance to speak with you. The news of these thefts must have been very hard for you. How are you doing?"

"Fine, thanks, miss." The snitching staircase was mercifully silent. If she could just make it back to the cupboard before Mrs Clod returned. . .

Miss Richards studied her, frowning slightly. "I'm confident the trouble with the police will pass, Freya, so you mustn't worry about that. But the loss of the Dragons must be hard. Your father will keep his award, I'm sure. His good fortune finding those *magnificent*. . ."

"I'm not upset about that, honestly," Freya lied. "It's not important."

It came out a little more forcefully than she had intended. Miss Richards raised her eyebrows. "Maybe not to you, Freya. Some people might be very envious of your father's prize."

There was a short silence. Freya was hoping that if she didn't say anything, the conversation would be over. Miss Richards, meanwhile, seemed to have tripped over a loose thought, and lost herself in reverie for a moment.

Then she sighed. "Well," she said, "I'd better get back to Crossword Club, and you had better get back to your chores. But any time you want to talk . . . I'm here."

"Thanks, miss!" said Freya. She gave the history mistress a manic grin. Then she bolted for freedom, and pounded back down the stairs.

To her relief, the cupboard was Clod-free. She darted in, and reached for the pile of papers, her heart clattering in her chest—

—but the envelope, and the sketches inside, had gone.

That night, Mrs Clod did not go rummaging in the bins.

The only ones rummaging were the ants. The ants kept coming, in a great line, as if they were following a path – and, in a way, they were. Ants that had gone to the bins before had oozed chemicals from their bodies, called pheromones, and left a trail of them behind. The smell of those chemicals meant, food over here. So all the other ants were walking along wafting at the ground with their antennae, which they use to smell – like long wavy noses – and following the trail up to the bins.

Imagine what they found when they arrived. If you are the size of an ant, a whole bin full of food must be an incredible sight.

Mrs Clod hadn't been following pheromones. Science has not yet explained Mrs Clod.

The twins' story

That night, Freya couldn't sleep. She ached all over from her day of cleaning, and she was exhausted, but wide awake. She sat in her bed, thinking.

If somebody had sketched the locks and keys, it stood to reason somebody had *made* those keys. There was the cutting machine right there, after all. That meant that somebody else had a set of keys to each building – except the school, for which they had keys *to the Dragon's case*. It had to be. What else in the school had three locks?

Surely, then, the mystery artist was the thief! But who were they? And how on earth had they seen inside all those locks?

The sketches were in Mrs Clod's cupboard. And Mrs Clod *did* like to make keys. In a way, then, she was the obvious choice. But something was niggling at Freya: Mrs Clod was the one who had made the three keys to the school's Dragon in the first place. She wouldn't have needed a sketch for those – she already had them. It didn't quite add up.

The other papers in the pile were Henny's, as far as Freya had seen. So, she thought, it would make sense if the sketches belonged to Henny, too. That seemed possible.

But. Neither Mrs Clod nor Henny could have snatched the papers away again that afternoon. There was no doubt that the papers were gone: Mrs Clod had been gone a long time rescuing the carpet, so Freya had thoroughly searched the cupboard. Only Miss Featherly and Miss Richards had had a chance to grab them – she hadn't heard anybody else on the staircase. And why would anybody but the thief know about those sketches, or want to take them?

Freya thought of Miss Featherly jealously guarding her locked drawer of pencil-covered papers – had she spotted what was missing, perhaps, while looking for her poem? Perhaps it wasn't only Henny whose private papers Mrs Clod was hoarding.

She drew the duvet tighter around herself, and thought furiously. All four of those mistresses had been up and about on the night of the theft: Miss Featherly off "bat-watching", Henny in her study, Miss Richards actually *looking right at* the school's Dragon, and Mrs Clod rummaging in the bins. That was strange behaviour from all of them. Except perhaps Henny, who was just habitually strange.

So any of them could be the thief.

She occupied herself with these thoughts, and tried not to think about the alternative theory: that the twins took the Dragons. She was also steadfastly not thinking about their offer to meet her at midnight. Or she was trying not to.

As midnight drew closer, all these thoughts got more and more tangled, until they stopped really being thoughts at all and just became a mess. When there are too many things you just don't know, thinking doesn't help much.

At three minutes to midnight, she began pacing the room.

At midnight, she went to stare out of the window. She stayed there for five minutes. Nothing happened. The hollow, empty feeling of the school seemed to be magnified tonight.

At ten past midnight she got back into bed and curled up into a little ball, trying to make the thoughts stop tangling themselves any further. She felt disappointed, but she couldn't say what she had been expecting exactly. She shut her eyes.

There was a knock at the door.

It was so faint that at first Freya wondered whether she had imagined it. But it came a second time, more firmly; so she got up, padded to the door, and opened it. In the dark hallway there were two small shadows.

"Hi! Is it just you in here? Is it safe to come in?" whispered the first.

"Hello," whispered the second.

And without waiting to be invited, the shadows came inside. Freya turned on her lamp, and the Stone twins blinked at her.

"How did you. . .?" she hissed.

"There's a coal cellar cover outside the front gate," said Daniel. "You can get into the main cellars from there. They lead out into the dining hall. And there's a map of the school in the head's office which we used to find your room."

"You were in *Miss Henderson's office?*" Freya said, forgetting to whisper.

"It's OK, no one saw us. And now we're here."

They certainly were. Esmie tucked herself up on the window seat, looking very much at home, while Daniel paced in front of the empty fireplace as though he owned the place.

"Freya," Esmie said, "it wasn't us who stole the Dragons. Do you believe us?"

Freya hesitated. She wanted to, but the twins *had* just broken into the school via the coal cellar and located her room in the middle of the night. She sank on to her bed.

"I don't know," she said.

"Well, it wasn't us, we promise," said Daniel. "But it's only a matter of time before someone finds out we were there. We've already had a police officer call our dad about all the bats, wanting help getting at the roosts. He's clocked that they woke up in all the buildings that had a Dragon. Which I *do* think is weird. There must be a reason, don't you think?"

He paused, as if hoping Freya might have some thoughts on PC Fig and the Mystery of the Waking Bats. She did not.

"Anyway," Daniel went on, unperturbed, "the phone call made us nervous. We need to find the real thief before we get into trouble."

"You think *you're* in trouble," said Freya bitterly. "They found my dad's keys outside the museum. I was meant to hand them in, he was so worried about them getting lost. When he hears. . ." She only had two days now until he arrived at the school and found the Dragons missing. And that was assuming that Miss Henderson didn't find an excuse to call him and rat on her earlier. Freya hadn't decided yet whether she could face telling him the whole story about the twins. It would be awful to tell him – but awful, too, to have such a huge secret wedged between them.

Esmie's eyes widened, and Daniel exclaimed, "Oh *no*! Do they think it was *you*? What happened?"

So Freya started to explain. She had meant to ask *them* to do the explaining, but once she had started telling her side of the story, she found couldn't stop. She told them about DI North, and the demerits, and the day cleaning with Mrs Clod, and the key sketches, and the way they had just gone missing. She told them about the four mistresses who might own the sketches, and their strange movements that night. She sidestepped her lingering suspicion that maybe this was all irrelevant, and the twins were the real culprits; but she poured out all of the rest of it. And all the way through, they just nodded and blinked and blinked and nodded.

"So it was someone in the school then, Daniel," said Esmie, looking at him pointedly.

"Why?" said Freya. "Who did *you* think it was?"

Daniel was pacing again. "Throg Three," he said.

"*What*? They're *his* Dragons. Why would he steal from himself?"

Esmie shrugged wearily, but Daniel was unabashed. "I don't know, but he's got the only other full set of keys, hasn't he? And he wears them on a belt, apparently, even at *night*, so no one can take them. And we don't think it was *you*, so I thought that only left him. But if someone in this school made a third set... I wonder who..." Daniel paused pacing triumphantly. "Miss Henderson! I bet it was her! She's *awful*."

"Daniel," said Esmie, "Freya's *told* us who the suspects are."

"Miss Henderson was at a hotel miles away, anyway," said Freya.

"So she *says*."

"The detective is checking up on alibis. It was the

first thing she was going to do." Freya thought, but didn't add, that DI North wasn't stupid; and Daniel was not the Great Detective he thought himself to be. She could feel her temper rising. He had not yet thought to ask how she was feeling, or say sorry for the trouble she was in.

"Well," said Daniel, "we'll put her down as a maybe. Ooh, what about the head girl? Didn't you say she hates you and your dad? It could be her! Or," he added, *very* solemnly, "there's always the *curse*."

It was like the night in the museum. He was racing ahead doing his own thing, and there was no stopping him.

"Freya," said Esmie firmly, "Why don't you tell us *why* those four mistresses might have done it."

Freya shot her a grateful look, and tried to put her mounting irritation aside. She had been turning this question over, too. "Well, they're worth a lot of money, obviously," she said, "and money is a motive for anyone. But Miss Richards was definitely the most excited about the Dragons – old English stuff is her passion. She's pretty serious about it, she's written papers on runes and stuff in the journals my dad reads. And earlier today she was being a bit weird, saying 'some people' might be envious of him. . . I wasn't really paying attention, but I've been wondering about it since.

"Then, Henny keeps asking to be allowed to examine the Dragons – she thinks there might be an explanation for the curse stories. I don't know if that's a reason to take them, really. But I can believe she might have *borrowed* them, then accidentally blown them up or something." Freya ticked these off on her fingers: two down. "Then Miss Featherly. She's not interested in the Dragons at all. Or at least, she never *seemed* to be. But I've been thinking; she's always got flashy jewellery on, and her study's full of really expensive-looking stuff. None of the other teachers seem to have that much cash. How's she buying it all? Stealing?"

Daniel nodded thoughtfully. "And Mrs Clod?"

Freya sighed, at a loss for how to explain Mrs Clod. "No idea," she said, "but it *was* her cupboard, so we really ought to consider it. Money?"

"OK," said Daniel. His pacing was increasingly frenetic, and increasingly annoying. "The first thing to do is search for these keys, then, or the sketches at least. You said the police are searching everything leaving the school? So they've got to still be here. We might as well start with the studies of those four mistresses, right? I think we should look into Miss Henderson and Abigail too. We could—"

"Wait," said Freya, in a forceful voice she didn't know she had. It was *very* forceful. Both the twins looked at her, wide-eyed.

"I'm in a lot of trouble," she said, in the new voice. "And you can't just break into my school and start telling me how to deal with it. If I get in any more trouble, Miss Henderson is calling my dad and telling him everything." She glared at Daniel. He had been hurrying her along in his river way, but she wasn't going to let him. "You still haven't answered any of *my* questions. I don't really know that *you* aren't the thieves yet."

Daniel opened his mouth, but Esmie got in first. "What would you like to know?"

This was a good question. "Um," said Freya, her forceful voice faltering. "Well, for starters – Daniel, you said you saw someone in the museum that night. It must have been the thief." *If you're telling the truth*, she added in her head. "What did you see exactly?"

A new expression snuck on to Daniel's face. He *almost* looked embarrassed. "It sounds a bit weird, to be honest," he said.

He looked at Esmie, as though for encouragement, but she was taking a great interest in her knees.

"Well," he said, "I'll tell you it exactly how I remember it. I'd just caught Nimrod when I heard footsteps approaching the exhibition room, so I turned off my torch and started creeping out towards the other door. But before I got there, the – well, the Dragon, it – it started glowing."

He paused. There was a very silent silence.

"It was sort of a bluish colour," he clarified. "Then I tripped over a rope, and I heard this whispering voice say something like 'Outta here!' And then I ran."

Freya's heart sank. She had never heard anything that sounded less like the truth in all her life.

"I'm sure there's an explanation," said Daniel uneasily. "Don't you think? Oh!" – and his eyes went very round – "Freya, is there anything about the Dragons glowing in the curse legends?"

Freya did not answer this. Her fists were clenched at her sides. "That's it?" she said at last. "*That's* your story?"

Daniel's chin rose defiantly. "It's the truth."

Suddenly, Freya felt like crying. The whole thing was ridiculous. She could not believe that any of this was happening.

But Daniel didn't notice, of course. "Come on, there isn't time for this. We need to get searching."

Freya looked from Daniel to Esmie and back, not knowing *what* to believe.

"Freya," said Esmie. "We didn't do it. I promise." She sat forward on the window seat, wide eyes serious. "Anyway – look at it this way. If we're the thieves, you're in trouble, and there's nothing to be done. But if we're *not*, and someone else has another set of keys, you need to find them. Fast. Before your dad comes back and hears the whole story – right? And you can't search all four studies properly by yourself tonight – it will take for ever."

This was a long speech for Esmie. Freya was a bit taken aback. But it *did* seem to make sense. She only had two days before the party.

"I'm so sorry about all the trouble you're in," Esmie added. "I really am. We want to help. What harm can we do now, anyway? Do the mistresses have anything worth stealing in their studies?"

"I don't know. I doubt it."

"Then what's the risk? Let us help."

She stared at Freya, big eyes wide and solemn. Daniel stopped pacing to join in the staring. It was very intense. Freya couldn't think straight.

"All right," she said at last, "all right. Fine. But *I'm* in charge, OK? You'll search where I tell you. And don't take any risks."

Even she knew that this was a stupid thing to say. The whole thing was a risk. They just had to do it anyway. There was a short silence.

"It *is* weird, isn't it," said Daniel, "the way the bats woke up this week? In all the buildings! It's like they knew something was up."

Freya didn't bother to reply to that. This was not the time to be worrying about bats. She stood, and summoned her new forceful voice again, although inside she was more tangled up than ever.

"OK," she said. She tried to clutch the keys: her fists closed on nothing. "Here's the plan."

The twins had brought three torches with ten different brightness settings, and they showed Freya how to use them. They told her to shut the curtains first and demonstrated how to make sure your torch beam didn't hit the window – like nice, normal, non-criminal-mastermind children.

Lights flashed and dimmed and swirled and flared. For the moth, still crouched above, the world had suddenly stopped making any sense at all. He waved his antennae in confusion, and decided maybe it was time to go and have a nice lie-down.

The snitching staircase

Before they reached the snitching staircase, Freya made Daniel take a vow of silence.

The staircase was in darkness. Good. They kept close to the enormous pillar, pressing against the wall for support in the shadows.

At the first door, Freya stopped, and pointed at the sign on it: MISS RICHARDS.

Esmie nodded, and went inside.

Freya and Daniel spiralled a little further down, then she pointed again: MISS FEATHERLY.

Daniel nodded three times, gave her a thumbs up, saluted, and held up crossed fingers for luck. The vow of silence was clearly killing him. Then he slipped inside.

Mrs Clod's cupboard was locked, eight times. Freya wasn't going to be able to search it again. This was annoying; but at least, thought Freya, she had had a good amount of time in there earlier.

That just left Henny's study. The light was off tonight. Freya went inside and shut the door.

First she crossed to the window, and shut the curtains as the twins had instructed. Then she switched on the torch, on its dimmest setting. She trailed the beam of light across the darkness, trying to make sense of Henny's study. She had never been inside it before.

The room was crammed with an unbelievable amount of *stuff*. A lot of it seemed to be bizarre inventions, old junk covered in dials and limbs and lenses and cogs and springs. In amongst this there were papers and mugs and dying houseplants and lost cardigan buttons and paperbacks of Millicent Leatherby the space-cowgirl detective; the overall effect was like one giant *oh dear*.

It was a terrible place to look for seven pieces of paper and a set of keys. But surrounded by all of Henny's inventions, Freya couldn't help feeling those sketches really might be hers; she had no idea how somebody had worked out the insides of all those locks, but it seemed like the sort of thing Henny would be able to pull off.

There was nothing for it but to get to work, inch by inch. Freya's mind started to run ahead to where else she and the twins ought to look, but then the scale of the task began to panic her. So she shut those thoughts out, and concentrated.

She focused on nothing but her search: her world narrowed to the end of her torch beam. She moved in slow motion, carefully sifting through the clutter, doing her best not to make a sound.

The inventions were fascinating. But there was no time to dawdle. So she steadfastly ignored the kettle with three antennae, the ticking compass attached to a wire circuit, and the mangled remains of what looked suspiciously like a partially exploded engine.

There were stacks of scribbled papers by Henny too, with mysterious titles like *On the Radiative Properties of Supernovae* and *Sonoscopes: A Practical Treatise* and *The Soundscape of Chiroptera*. Freya moved fast through these, although she *did* pause over one set of papers headed *Accounting for the "Curse" of the Eldrida Dragons*.

She crouched down on the floor a moment to read these. Henny had come up with a whole raft of theories, detailing possible traces of poisons or dangerous substances that could have been painted over the Dragons or hidden inside them, which would make all seven together cause sickness or fires... But next to several she had scrawled *Need to X-ray Dragon*, or *Would have to subject to high heat to be sure*, or in one case *Smash one open to check?*

So she *was* still thinking about the curse question – and quite seriously, it seemed. There was no doubt that any scientific discovery about the beloved Dragons and their curse would make Henny a shoo-in at the Society. Had she perhaps tried these tests last night – with disastrous consequences?

But this was not evidence. Freya needed to find the keys to the Dragons' homes, or at least the sketches of the keys, if she was going to convince DI North that her dad's keys were not the only way in. And convince herself, too: the image of Daniel fleeing the museum with a bucket held aloft kept floating up, unwanted. She straightened up again and moved her little circle of light onwards to the next pile, carving a new slice out of the thick dark.

As night wore on, she felt a rising panic. There was so much here, and she wasn't making headway fast enough. From the wall, Lord Throgmorton watched her from yet another portrait, amused as ever.

There was a clock on Henny's desk, but it must have had its insides tampered with, because Freya was thoroughly taken aback when she heard the first bird piping to itself outside. It was still dark. What time was it?

Then, suddenly, her light cut out. Her torch battery had gone.

"Oh, *no*," she breathed. She hardly dared move without it: one wrong move in this room could send everything tumbling. For a minute she just stood in the darkness, listening to the bird. What now?

There was the whisper of the door behind her, and

she spun around in horror: but a beam of torchlight revealed Esmie.

"Oh, you scared me," whispered Freya.

"Sorry. Any luck?"

"No. And my torch battery has gone. You?"

"Nothing. Miss Richards is tidy. I read some of the stuff she's written about the Dragons – she's pretty into them, isn't she?" She swept her torch around the chaos of the room. "What a mess. We should all be helping in here," she said. "I'll get Daniel. Hold on." She shone her light at the desk, and pointed out, "There's a torch on top of those papers." Then she was gone.

Freya picked up and tried the torch, but it was as broken as everything else. So she stayed standing still, and held on. More birds had joined the first, and around the edges of the curtain, she saw the faint silver beginnings of dawn.

A few minutes later, the door breathed open again, and two shadows entered. "Oh wow," whispered Daniel, "it *is* messy. Esmie said it was."

"Did you find anything in Miss Featherly's office?" asked Freya, without much hope.

"No sketches, no keys. But that drawer was still locked, the one you said she was cagey about. *And* I found *this*." He handed Freya a crumpled note. "What do you think?"

Freya read:

I borrowed your binoculars on Thursday night, and what I saw through them was very interesting. I think you know what I mean. I will keep your secret if you will. Keep mine. DO WE HAVE A DEAL?

Freya's hope ballooned rapidly once more. "So someone saw Miss Featherly doing something on Thursday night. It must have been to do with the theft! It *must!*" She thought for a moment. "*I will keep your secret if you will keep mine.* What secret? No signature. . . I wonder who. . ." She stared at the note, as though willing herself to see an answer in it. "Shall we take it to DI North?"

Before anyone could reply, there was an impatient banging on the study door.

All three children froze.

The banging came again.

"Clarissa! Clarissa, I can see your light! Open up, woman."

For a moment, Freya's heart stopped altogether.

Miss Henderson.

Freya did not know what kind of birds were singing outside, and she didn't especially care.

The first, a hearty whistle, was a blackbird. The higher peep-peeping that came next was a robin, and then they were joined by two wrens who prrrped like tiny alarm clocks. They were all announcing their arrival, and their whereabouts. It was like a map of all the garden's birdlife, in song.

Freya was busy. She didn't need a map of all the garden's birdlife in song, just then. Still, it's there every morning, just in case anybody wants it.

Lord Joseph Edward Throgmorton the Third

There was approximately one-and-a-half seconds of silence, during which Freya's mind went on a wild roller coaster of realizations.

She realized that being found in the study was bad. She realized that the twins being found in the study was worse. She realized that there was nowhere to hide, and that her choices were to be discovered alone, or discovered with the twins.

That was an easy choice. She was across the room to the door at top speed, and opened it to find Miss Henderson's fist raised mid-knock.

"Um. Good morning, miss." Freya stepped out, ducking under the raised fist, and pulled the door safely shut behind her.

Miss Henderson stood frozen in outrage. Only her tongue moved, a little flicker of shock. After a moment, she slowly lowered the fist.

"Henny – I mean, Miss Henderson – isn't there, miss. I wanted to see her. I have questions about. . . um" – Freya wracked her brains for anything remotely sciencey – "um, bats. Ultrasound."

The headmistress just stared at her, even more outraged by this blatant display of *thinking*.

Freya took a deep breath and tried to take Daniel's approach to conversation. "I'm really interested in ultrasound, and echolocating. You know, like bats do. And, um, how sonar works. And Henny said I should see her outside class hours. So. . ."

It was lucky, Freya thought, that she had a track record of too many curious questions. Miss Henderson continued to glare, but although she seemed furious, she did not seem suspicious. "Freya," she said at last. "Go to my office."

Freya hesitated. It would mean leaving the twins in the study.

"*Now.*"

She forced herself to walk away and let out a breath of relief as Miss Henderson came spidering after her. They reached the headmistress's study just as the bell rang to summon everyone out of their beds and down to breakfast; it was even later than Freya had guessed.

To her enormous relief, Henny was waiting at the headmistress's door. So that was both sisters out of the way, for now.

"Oh, Annabel, there you are," said Henny. "I've been – oh – hello, Freya."

"I just found Freya trespassing in your study, Clarissa. The sheer *nerve*... Freya, what's that in your hand?"

Freya had been so preoccupied, she had totally forgotten about the torch. Thankfully she had balled the blackmail note up tight in her clenched fist; she slipped it into her pocket now. "Oh. Um. Sorry, miss," she said to Henny. "I borrowed your torch."

"Not to worry, Freya. Annabel, can I speak to you?"
Henny turned breathlessly to her sister.

"What is it?"

"It's, um, oh dear. . . It's little Felicity's parents. They
called. They're terribly cross about her shoe dissolving
in Science Club, and I'm not sure what to say. . ."

"I will be *thrilled* to discuss Felicity's shoe," said Miss
Henderson. "Later."

"Yes, of course. It's just that I have to take the third
form for their Sunday Joy-of-Nature Appreciation Walk
first thing after breakfast."

"Fine," said Miss Henderson through gritted teeth.
"Fine. I wanted a word with you too, as it happens. Miss
Timms says you may have *borrowed* a piano string? A
low C?"

Henny blushed furiously. "Ah – a small experiment –
she hardly ever uses that note, you see. . ."

"Well, it seems she wishes to use it now. You can tell
me your excuses in a moment. I will deal with Freya
first." She marched into the study, leaving the door open
behind her for them both to follow.

Meekly, Henny and Freya filed into the office. Miss

Henderson had her back to them, pouring herself a glass of water. Freya hovered uncertainly by a spindly silver chair, unsure whether to sit. Outside, clattering feet made their way to breakfast, in another world.

Water tinkled into cut crystal for an eternity, then Miss Henderson turned. She looked more collected, although her hand still shook with controlled rage. "Since you arrived at this school, Freya, you have refused to abide by its spirit. You clearly do not appreciate the opportunity you have been given. Trespassing in a teacher's office is the last straw. I will be speaking to the Trust." She sipped her water, and licked her lips. "I think," she said, "that we need to reconsider whether you belong at this school."

Freya's stomach lurched. Miss Henderson was trying to have her expelled! Even though she hated Throgmorton's, she hated the idea of her dad's shock and disappointment even more. *Expelled!*

"Oh, goodness," murmured Henny. "Do you think that's really. . ."

Miss Henderson cut her off with a cold look.

"Yes," said Miss Henderson coldly. "I do."

There was a few seconds' silence. Miss Henderson's bulging eyes never left Freya, and she licked her lips with enormous satisfaction.

Then PC Fig popped his head round the door and said cheerfully, "Morning, Miss M! Visitor for you!"

Miss Henderson breathed deeply. "Not now. Please tell them to go away, Mr Fig."

"Right you are." Figs's head disappeared, and they heard him announce, "She says go away."

"She says WHAT?" roared a voice. It was a rich, deep voice. Miss Henderson went pale.

The door banged open, and someone swept inside.

There was no mistaking him. He had his ancestor's nose, although not the humorous mouth; instead his little mouth rested in a pout, before puddling downwards into a magnificent chin. With one great hand, he clasped a black cane, which he leaned on heavily. One blue eye glowered at them all, while the other drooped downwards, as though it had grown weary of the world a long time ago.

Lord Joseph Edward Throgmorton the Third.

"Your Lordship!" cried Miss Henderson. She used

a tinkling little voice Freya had never heard before. "You're early – we weren't expecting you until tomorrow—"

"I am never *early* at my own school, Annabel," he boomed. "I arrive when I choose. I have come about my Dragons."

"Of course. Would you—"

"As if the humiliation of the theft was not sufficient, I have now been informed that the staff and students of *my school* are under investigation."

Miss Henderson smiled a strained little smile to match the tinkling voice. "Yes, it is very unfortunate—"

"Are you running a school or a crime ring, woman?"

"Your Lordship," the headmistress oozed, "please, do sit down. I'm very glad you're here. This child" – Freya was, to her alarm, suddenly the focus of Miss Henderson's bejewelled finger and Throg Three's glowering eye – "is the cause of the shameful investigations taking place at this school. This is Freya Robinson, Dr Robinson's child. As you know I objected to her placement in this school, as I feared that her wild upbringing would make her quite unsuitable. I was correct. I intend to call her father at once, and have her removed—"

"You will do no such thing," Throg Three barked. "Nobody will be calling Dr Robinson about *anything* until those Dragons have been found."

"But Your Lordship, I have just discovered that she is a common little thief. She has stolen my sister's *torch*." Even Miss Henderson could tell that "torch" was not a brilliantly dramatic ending. She pointed extra dramatically at the torch to make up for it.

"I was just borrowing it," said Freya, appealing to Henny. "Anyway," she added, "it's broken." She turned it on. "See."

"That's not broken," said PC Fig. He took the torch from Freya, examining it with interest. "Yup, thought so. It's an ultraviolet light. We use those in the force. To check if a bank note is forged, you know."

Trust Henny to have a weird ultraviolet torch instead of a normal useful one. Throg Three glared at the torch, and then at PC Fig. The silence would have been impressive, if it hadn't been ruined by Henny whispering, "Annabel, if I could, Felicity's shoe. . ."

Lord Throgmorton the Third cleared his throat. "I must be very dense, Miss Henderson. What does this child and this torch have to do with my Dragons?"

"What I am trying to say, Your Lordship," said Miss Henderson, "is that Freya has caused havoc—"

"Havoc," announced Throg Three, banging the desk, "is what children cause. I am not remotely interested. Unless you are suggesting that *she* stole my Dragons?" He turned to PC Fig. "Officer, is there any indication that this girl is a suspect?

"She's on the list," said PC Fig cheerfully, putting the torch down on the desk and feeling for something in his pocket. "Here we go. Highly suspicious. Had the keys to each of the buildings the dragons were stolen from. Grudge against the school, sounds like. But *I* think it was the bats." There was a collective groan, but PC Fig didn't notice; he was busy unfolding a page from his notebook. "I've calculated how many average bats it would take to lift the different size Dragon statues, and I've been in touch with Mr Stone from the conservation trust to find out where the roosts are. I haven't been able to leave my post to look yet, but I get a morning off tomorrow." He held out a sheet of paper covered in scrawled sums. "Here, take a look, Your Lordship."

Lord Joseph Edward Throgmorton the Third cleared his throat, and did not look at the sums. PC Fig fell silent. There was a tense pause.

"Everybody out," said Throg Three, "except the headmistress. I would like a private word, *without* idiotic interruptions."

The others didn't need telling twice. Freya hurried outside. Then she found that her legs didn't want to hold her up any more, and she sat down suddenly at the foot of the empty plinth.

The Dragons were still missing. She was no closer to finding the thief. It looked very much like she was going to be expelled. And tomorrow her dad would be here.

The others looked down at her in concern. Henny asked if she was feeling all right, and PC Fig offered her a toffee. But Freya was catastrophically not all right, and she didn't think toffee would help. The smells of breakfast coming from the assembly hall were making her feel distinctly queasy.

"So," said PC Fig, after a few moments of strained silence. "Why d'you have an ultraviolet torch, miss?"

Henny was checking her watch, and murmuring worriedly about dissolving shoes and nature walks; but at this she looked up, eyes alight. "Ah, it's for my research, PC Fig. I am investigating the properties of light waves and sound waves at the ultra and infra ends of the spectrum, you see. Ultrasound, ultraviolet, and so on. *Very* interesting."

"Yes! It must be. And," he added, with a wink, "very successful, I hear on the grapevine."

This was puzzling; Freya wasn't sure if he was making fun of Henny with this last remark. She didn't seem sure what to do with it either. She blushed, and *oh dear*ed, and looked at her watch again. "Well. Um. If the headmistress is going to be a while, perhaps I should pop to my study and—"

The twins. Freya leapt to her feet in panic. "Wait!" she cried, startling PC Fig so much that he choked on his toffee. "That *did* sound interesting, what you were saying about ultrathingy, miss. Ultraviolet. What – er – what is it?"

146

"Well, Freya," said Henny, slapping PC Fig on the back, "it's a kind of light wave. Light travels in waves, you see, and bounces off things into our eyes, and that's how we see. But ultraviolet waves are very short waves that our eyes can't detect. Just like ultrasound is very high sound that our ears can't detect."

"But it makes some things glow in the dark," said PC Fig, eyes watering. "We use it to know if a bank note is real – if it is, it will have a mark on it that glows in UV light. And there are other things that glow too – teeth and ivory, and spinach, and some stones, and apparently scorpions do it – isn't that right, Miss M?"

"Yes, yes," said Henny, looking dreamily delighted by the very thought of all that glowing spinach. "It's called *fluorescing*."

Freya didn't care *what* it was called. She was staring at the two of them, mind reeling. Ivory? Ivory glowing in the dark? Was *that* what Daniel had seen that night in the museum? The statue *had* been glowing!

"So your torch makes things flour-whatsit?" she asked.

"Fluoresce. Yes. It—" But before Henny could finish,

the door to Miss Henderson's office opened, and Throg Three emerged. Henny fell silent at once.

"I will be back," His Lordship announced, "when I have spoken to this DI North woman. Maybe I'll get some sense out of her." And he began wading across the entrance hall, stick thumping. When he drew level with the three of them, he paused, and fixed his good eye on Freya.

"We will find the Dragons," he told her, "and my celebration tomorrow will proceed. But more importantly, we *will* find the thief, and there *will* be Justice. JUSTICE!" He took a moment to recover from this last word, then continued, leaning forward heavily on his stick. "I hope for your sake," he said, "that you were not involved, Miss Robinson. And for your father's sake, too."

Freya nodded, a very small nod.

Throg Three considered her a moment longer. Then he went wading off again, and with a bang of the front door, he was gone.

"Annabel, *might* I have a word?" said Henny.

"Fine, fine, Clarissa," said Miss Henderson from

her doorway. "Come in, then." Her gaze fell on Freya. "Freya, go to your room and stay there. And out of trouble, please."

Freya nodded again, but she had no intention of going to her room. She said goodbye to PC Fig, who resumed his seat at the front door. Then she walked as calmly as she possibly could up the staircase.

As soon as she was out of sight, she broke into a run.

Her mind raced as fast as her legs. So Daniel's strange story was true! The thief had to be able to find the Dragon in the dark. An ultraviolet torch's beam wouldn't be visible to anyone passing the museum's windows – but it would make the ivory Dragon glow.

And Henny had an ultraviolet torch. Had she been the one using it for the thefts, or had someone known about it and taken it?

Whoever it was, it proved one thing: Daniel's crazy story hadn't been a lie. Someone else really had been there that night. The twins were innocent. They were her friends.

It didn't solve their problem, of course. But even so, Freya felt suddenly infinitely lighter.

For some reason, as she ran, she remembered Moriarty in his bucket, flapping and calling to no one; and flying up the stairs, she felt as he had looked that night in the garden, taking off into the wide-open darkness – free to find his way home.

Freya was not the only one who had found something exciting to tell her friends. A single honeybee, finding that the fog had cleared and the day was mild, had left the huddle of vibrating bees in her nest and gone to seek food.

And she had found some. *In winter!*

This news was so good that she had hurried back to her nest, and was now doing a dance. It was a very complicated dance, wiggling her furry little body about, and all the other bees watched with great interest – because the dance was telling them all about the food, and where to find it. Beekeepers call this a waggle dance.

Freya was going to use her voice, not a waggle dance, to share her news; but you can imagine that she danced, if you like. It comes to the same thing.

The sonoscopes

Freya burst back in to Henny's study. There was no one there.

"Psst," she whispered. "It's me! You can come out now."

There was a pause, and then the twins came crawling out from their hiding place under the desk. They looked worried, which didn't suit them. Freya realized that she had never seen them in daylight before. The light seeping round the curtains made them look faded, and somehow smaller.

"Hi!" whispered Daniel. "Can we still get out through the dining hall? Or the normal way?"

"The dining hall will be busy. Breakfast's just finishing, then it gets used for choir. And the normal way takes you through the entrance hall, where PC Fig is. Best we stay for a bit."

"What if Henny comes back?"

"She's got to take the third form for a walk now, and they'll be out all morning," said Freya. "We're probably safer here than anywhere." She hoped this was true, because she couldn't think of another option. She dropped to the floor next to them. "And I found out something."

She told them all about the torch, and ultraviolet light, and fluor-whatsit. Four solemn eyes got wider and wider as she talked.

"So the statue *was* glowing," said Daniel. "It was UV light."

Freya nodded. "I believe you now. I'm sorry." The others just blinked, which seemed to mean it was all right. Freya smiled at them, and continued. "We've still got until the party tomorrow to crack this – Throg Three is making Miss Henderson keep quiet, for now. Right, then. Whoever our thief is, we're pretty sure they sketched the locks – somehow; made a spare set of keys; then used this torch. And they might have said 'Outta here'." She faltered; hearing this out loud, it did not seem so impressive. "Er – I'm not sure it adds up to much yet."

For a moment her light-feeling almost drained away, with a sickening twist of her stomach, as though somebody had pulled a plug. She was suddenly very aware of her sleepless, breakfastless state; of the sickly grey light in the curtained study; of the footsteps outside as girls trickled away from breakfast, talking and laughing, in another world.

But as her excitement nosedived, the twins were just getting started. "It's Henny's torch," said Daniel eagerly. "Surely that makes her our prime suspect? Let's search the study again!"

"Sure, but remember the blackmail note to Miss Featherly," said Esmie. "She was up to *something* that night. And anyone could have borrowed the torch, right?"

"Let's have another look at the note," said Daniel.

Freya pulled herself together. She was tired, she told herself: that was all. And there was work to do. She took the paper out of her pocket, unfolded it, and read the words *On a morning full of crushing guilt at the consequences of my carelessness.*

"Oh, hang on, that's not it," she said. She put down the poem, found the note in her other pocket and smoothed it out.

The three of them stared at the poem and the note, side by side.

They were in the same handwriting.

Daniel rocked forward on his knees and studied them both eagerly. "Who wrote the poem, Freya?"

"Miss Featherly," said Freya. She was trying to make sense of it. There was, after all, no name on the note. They had just assumed it was for Miss Featherly because they had found it in her study. "So the note wasn't *to* Miss Featherly – it was *from* her. She hadn't sent it yet."

Miss Featherly was the one blackmailing someone – or

planning to, at least.

Freya read the note again:

I borrowed your binoculars on Thursday night, and what I saw through them was very interesting. I think you know what I mean. I will keep your secret if you will. Keep mine. DO WE HAVE A DEAL?

"I even *saw* Miss Featherly going out that night with a pair of binoculars," said Freya, feeling foolish for not spotting this earlier. "She said she was going bat-watching."

"So," said Esmie, "whose were the binoculars? Who was she blackmailing?" And that was the million-dollar question. But none of them had a million-dollar answer.

"I saw binoculars in Miss Featherly's room. They

were pretty fancy," said Daniel. "Big brass things. Covered in dials and things."

"Any sign of who they belonged to?" asked Freya.

"I didn't really look for that. Maybe we should check."

So Freya got up, put her head around the door, checked that the staircase was clear, and scuttled up to Miss Featherly's office. It didn't take her long to spot the binoculars, nestled between a jewellery box and a crystal swan.

They felt familiar, which seemed odd. Miss Featherly had been slipping them into her handbag when they met on the stairs, and Freya had barely seen them. But she had definitely had seen peculiar binoculars like these before, somewhere.

Then it came to her. She *had* seen an almost-identical pair, on the night of the theft – but not in school.

All her excitement came flooding back. She picked them up, raced out of Miss Featherly's office, flew back up the stairs to Henny's door and hurried inside.

"We saw some just like these at the Society!" she said, as she burst in. "I remember reading the label.

They're called sonoscopes. Do you remember?"

The others blinked at her. "Um," said Esmie.

"They were in that hall with all the inventions." She thought for a moment. "*And* there are notes on Henny's desk about sonoscopes, I passed them earlier."

The others blinked at her some more. "What's a sono . . . sono-thing?" said Daniel.

"Dunno," said Freya, rifling through the mess at top speed to find Henny's notes about the strange binoculars. She thought of the Society, and the carvings over the door: *Audi sonum cosmi*. Listen to the sound of the universe. "*Sono* means to make a sound. And you see things with scopes – microscopes, telescopes. Maybe they see sound? But that doesn't make any sense. . ."

"Yes it does," said Esmie, starting to look interested. "That's what bats do."

Freya had found the stapled bundle of papers now. *Sonoscopes: A Practical Treatise*. It was all in Henny's sprawling writing, and appeared to be some kind of instruction manual, covered in notes and corrections. She peered at it in the half-light.

"It looks like she *invented* these things," she said.

"They've got to be hers then! So why was there a pair at the Society?"

"That's what they do if they make you a Fellow," said Daniel. "They make a copy of your big invention for the gallery."

Freya frowned. "They've made Henny a Fellow? That means she'll be leaving. Why hasn't she said anything?"

The others shrugged, not very interested in this. "No idea," said Daniel. "But if these are hers, then she's the one Miss Featherly was blackmailing."

"And the UV torch is hers, too," said Esmie. "She's the one!"

Daniel had picked up the sonoscopes and was looking through them. "They don't make things any bigger," he said. "What are they meant to *do*?"

Freya was reading furiously. "It looks like they . . . they make a noise . . . an ultrasonic noise, too high to hear. And when that sound bounces off things, they read the echoes. Like a bat does! Like sonar. Er – try that button. I think it turns on the sound."

There was a switch on the bridge between the two

eyepieces, and Daniel pressed it. Freya's human ears heard nothing, but Daniel exclaimed as the view through the scopes changed. He passed them to Freya to look.

It was the study, except that it was all in fine grey strokes, as though someone had sketched it with a pencil.

A picture built from echoes.

It had a quiet, eerie beauty. But still, Freya couldn't quite see the point of it.

She returned to Henny's notes, and read out loud. "Sound waves," she read, "have many advantages over light waves. First, they are not entirely blocked by solid objects, allowing us to 'see' objects that are otherwise blocked from our view. They are reflected differently by different substances, allowing an assessment of—"

"Wait," said Daniel. "What was that first one? Not blocked by solid objects? Are you saying these can *see through* things?"

"I think so. . ."

"Right, so it's a sort of sonar device," said Esmie, now reading over Freya's shoulder. "But it looks *incredibly* advanced. . . Can I see the next page, Freya?"

So Freya spread out the notes on the floor, moving teacups and Millicent Leatherby paperbacks aside; and Esmie pored over them, while Freya and Daniel took it in turns to experiment.

Daniel found the dial that told the sonoscopes to only listen to certain kinds of echo, so that you only saw things that were metal, or only wood, or only stone. Freya spent a mesmerizing few minutes turning the dial, watching the picture shift, and shift, and shift again, half-worlds and hidden worlds fluttering in and out of view.

It was Freya herself who found out how to see through solid objects. There was a delicate golden dial, with numbers around the edge. If she set the dial to 6, say, she would see whatever was six inches away, without anything in between. Freya pointed them at the wall and turned the dial up to 10. She could see right through the wall now to the staircase beyond, in that same sketchy whispering grey. It was, thankfully, empty.

One dial zoomed in or out; another made things sharper or more blurred. There was a button that flipped the image, first upside down, then back to front, then—

Freya squinted, confused. It took her a moment to understand this third rotation. When she pointed the scopes at Henny's pinboard on the wall, she saw this:

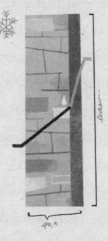

Then she understood. She was seeing a cross section – as though she had sliced the wall open, and looked at its insides. She turned to look at the keyhole – and there it was: the cross section of springs and pins needed to make the perfect key.

"*Look*," she said, passing it to the twins. "That's how the thief made the sketches of the locks." She didn't know why she was still saying "the thief", as if they didn't know who it was. It *had* to be Henny: her torch, and now her sonoscopes. It was just a little difficult to imagine.

"And she disturbed the bats doing it, with all the ultrasonic noise!" said Daniel. "I *knew* it was important that they all woke up like that. Brilliant, Freya." He frowned. "D'you think Miss Featherly looked through the sonoscopes and realized the same thing? And that's why she's blackmailing Henny?"

Freya looked doubtfully at the sonoscopes. Just owning them didn't seem like enough for blackmail. Wouldn't Miss Featherly need to know about the lock sketches, at the very least?

Esmie pointed at a button marked with a tiny engraving: *sonograph*. "What does this do?"

Freya pressed it. There was a flash, and a *whirrrr*, and a click; then another flash; then a slightly worrying bit of steam.

Cautiously, Freya looked through the lenses. There was a still image of what she had been pointing them at – like a photograph, but made from sound.

"Sonograph," murmured Esmie. "Like *photograph*. A sound photograph."

Freya tried it again: flash, *whirrr,* click, flash, slightly worrying steam. The old image had been replaced with a new one.

It seemed the sonoscopes could only store one image at a time. Freya thought hard. Henny must have brought each one home to make her sketches – one sonograph each night, each night disturbing a different roost of bats.

If Miss Featherly had borrowed the sonoscopes and seen the image of the lock, and put two and two together with the thefts. . .

Freya put the sonoscope back on to the see-through-things setting and looked around the room, seeing Miss Featherly's study above and the grounds outside through the curtains and—

"What?" said the twins, in unison, as Freya slowly lowered the sonoscopes.

Behind the painting of Lord Throgmorton was a hidden flight of steps. They led down under an archway, then curved off into a smudge of shadowy grey, out of sight.

"I might," said Freya, "have found you a way out."

Mice can hear ultrasound. A mouse which lived behind the skirting board in Henny's study was quivering madly, watching everything with bright little eyes.

She watched the strange children who had made the terrible noise, as they felt behind a painting for a hidden catch and loosened it. They discovered that this allowed the painting to roll sideways, revealing an archway behind.

She watched with relief as they went through it, almost shutting it, but not quite (after all, they didn't know what was in there, or whether they would be able to open it again from the inside). She was glad to see them gone.

But before the poor mouse could relax there was a fourth child, charging in a moment later, sure she had heard voices and not knowing she was only a moment too late to catch them. She didn't make the same racket, thankfully; but the mouse thought that the swing of her ponytail didn't look friendly.

The mouse decided, on balance, that it was a stay-at-home sort of day.

Under the surface

There were five stone steps behind the painting. Freya, Daniel and Esmie pattered down them. The steps led down to a tunnel going back the other way, crossing right underneath the room they had just come from; and then they stepped through an archway.

They were standing on a wide stone step, halfway up the most peculiar room Freya had ever seen. It was narrow, tall and circular, like the inside of a great chimney; and it stretched above and below them for what must have been the whole height of the school. Their step was part of a spiralling staircase which clung to the wall, circling round and round the room, down and down and down to a stone floor far below.

Equally far above, the ceiling was dotted with tiny pinprick windows to let in the light. The November sun cast speckled lights all over the floor, like soft grey stars.

They stood still, looking at it all in silence.

As they stood, there was a clattering of footsteps from outside the room, which echoed magnificently in the empty space; and Freya realized where they were.

"This is *inside* the snitching staircase." She was whispering, although she wasn't sure why. "Inside the pillar in the middle. That's why it's so loud out there. It's hollow at the centre."

Daniel was almost too full of questions to function. He just kept pointing at it all, and saying "Wha—?", which seemed to be all he could manage. Esmie was silent, but her eyes were even bigger than usual. They all set off down the stairs, taking care to press close to the cold stone on their right as they spiralled round the sides of the enormous room.

At last they reached the bottom. Here, a large wooden table stood in the middle of the space, occupying most of it. Shelves around the edges housed glass vials and scales and test tubes and great leather-bound books. It would have been cosy, except that the stone tower stretched above them to a dizzying height. In one corner another set of steps was set into the floor, descending downwards.

While Freya and Esmie stood in the strange starlight and stared, Daniel pattered down these steps to have a look, switching on his torch. "There are corridors going every direction down here," he called up. "Wow, it's a whole network of tunnels! I reckon these must go all over the school. . ." He kept talking, but his voice was getting fainter, and soon his footsteps and voice had faded out of earshot.

While Esmie made friends with some mice that had made a nest out of one of the books, Freya read the spines of the rest. *Essays on the Scientific Prediction of Weather Phenomena*, read one. *The Further Universe: A Treatise on the Undiscovered*, read another. Inside each somebody had written, in red ink, "J. E. Throgmorton."

So this had been Lord Throgmorton the First's private study. More of a laboratory, really. He must have had it built when he lived here. He looked like he had a sense of fun in his portraits, and now Freya knew that was true: you had to be fun to build yourself a web of hidden tunnels, with a secret starlit study at their heart.

For a moment, Freya forgot all about the stolen Eldrida Dragons and the keys. She felt unexpected tears starting. She had always thought there was nothing magical or mysterious at Throgmorton's. But all along, this had been here. Her father was right. You just had to look under the surface.

Daniel's head popped up from below, his small face alight with excitement. "Come and look at *this*," he said. Freya snapped back to attention, and Esmie left the mice (who had already grown fond of her, and squeaked after her sadly), and they followed him down the steps into the tunnels below.

He led them confidently through a befuddling set of twists and turns and ups and downs in the dark, his torchlight the only guide. No wonder the school hallways were so twisty and turny, if they were weaving around this other, hidden school. Freya really hoped Daniel knew what he was doing. Just as all the

twists and turns and darkness were starting to make her nervous, he stopped, and pointed his torch. "They *look* cursed, don't you think?" he said.

There was an alcove set into the wall. As the torch illuminated it, seven ghostly white figures stared back at them, their runes seeming somehow to shift and shimmer in the light.

The Seven Eldrida Dragons.

And a bunch of keys.

Freya smiled from ear to ear. *Got them.*

And then, like an echo, someone in the darkness crowed, "Got you!"

Freya couldn't see a thing outside the line of Daniel's torch, but she would know that voice anywhere.

"Freya Robinson," spat Abigail, "you are in *so* much trouble."

Abigail was not the only one who had discovered the intruders.

Below their feet there was a mole, who had also built a set of secret tunnels, underneath some of Lord Throgmorton's. His eyes were tiny and overhung with fur, and his ears were buried deep inside him behind his shoulders. But with his sensitive fur and his big paws and his quivering snout, he felt the world around him. The soil, moist or claggy or sandy or tickly-dry, and the quiver of the other creatures that moved through it, sending tiny vibrations through his world.

Three great humans clattering about sent most upsetting vibrations all through the mole's tunnel. He turned around grumpily and went back the way he had come.

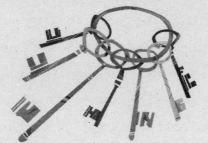

Through the wall

"I knew it," said Abigail's voice. "I *knew* you were the thief. So this is where you've been keeping them." She didn't have a torch of her own; she must have been following Daniel's distant light through the dark. Freya had to admit this was quite brave.

"I didn't put them here," said Freya. "We found them just now."

Abigail laughed, a single *ha*. "Is that the best story you've got? We'll see what DI North thinks of it when she hears it." She eyed Daniel and Esmie. "I'm sure she'll want to meet your friends too."

"It's true. We were going to tell the police," said

Freya. But she could suddenly see that from an outside perspective, she *did* look guilty. Abigail had caught her in a secret corridor with the missing Dragons, plus two intruders.

"Sure you were," said Abigail. "Well, you can explain it to DI North. But first I think I should go to Miss Henderson. I don't suppose you've bothered to read chapter nine of the Complete and Updated Book of Rules, but bringing strangers into the school will get you expelled straight away. You can pack your bags and go away with your famous father after the party tomorrow – *if* you haven't been arrested first."

"Who are you?" piped up Daniel. "Have you been looking for the Dragons too? Do you—"

"Daniel," hissed Freya. "Just be quiet, for one second. Abigail – listen to me – we've been trying to find out who stole the Dragons. We *were* at the museum that night, but—"

"Shh," said Esmie.

"I think we need to tell her the whole story," said Freya, "or else—"

"SHH," said Esmie.

"But she needs—"

Esmie stepped into the torch light, jabbed a finger at the wall opposite the Dragons and said, "I can hear something." Then she pressed her ear to the wall.

After a second's uncertainty, Daniel and Freya followed suit; and then Abigail too, unwilling to be left out of whatever was being overheard. Freya was surprised to feel wood instead of cold stone beneath her ear; and she could hear voices on the other side, so the wood was thin. They were, she guessed, behind another portrait. She pressed her ear close, and the voices magnified.

Somebody was crying, with great hiccuping sobs, and a cold voice was saying, ". . . For heavens' sake, pull yourself together, Clarissa."

Freya could see Abigail's half-lit face over the top of Daniel's head, and despite themselves, they exchanged a glance. It was their headmistress's voice. And Clarissa was Henny's name.

"I just thought," said the sobbing person – and Freya and Abigail locked eyes again, because it *was* unmistakably Henny – "if we put them somewhere – to be found – then no one would have to know. . ."

"Oh yes? You're willing to risk being caught with them, are you?"

Henny sobbed, but didn't reply.

"And," went on Miss Henderson, her voice muffled but audible, "*if* you somehow managed it unnoticed, do you really think His Lordship will have the investigation dropped? He's furious. He wouldn't let the thief off the hook just because they lost their nerve."

Henny let out a wail.

"Oh, calm down," said her sister. "They're not going to find them. I told you I've hidden them well – the keys too. The safest thing to do is to wait it out. Keep our heads down and wait for someone else to be arrested."

"But the investigation is pointing to poor little Freya. We *have* to come forward. Tell me where the statuettes are, Annabel – we *have* to give them back."

"Do we, Clarissa?" They had to press their ears extra hard, as Miss Henderson's voice grew dangerously soft here – like a spider spinning its final, deadly threads around a fly. "How would you propose to pay your debt without them? Or would you leave your own sister ruined, after all I've done to try to protect you?"

"Oh," said Henny. "Oh, d-dear" – and she blew her nose loudly.

"Oh!" breathed Daniel. *"Oh d-dear.* Not *outta here. That's* what I heard that night in the museum."

There was the scraping of a chair. "I have to go and meet with DI North in town – I'll be a couple of hours. Just hold your nerve until I can get those Dragons out of here and make the sale, Clarissa. That's all you have to do. Try not to let me down this time." They heard footsteps. "You can stay in here," said Miss Henderson, "while you pull yourself together. And don't forget about our meeting tonight. We need to get our stories straight."

There was a sniff. "Yes. Of course. Yes. Oh, and I do f-feel bad about cancelling the third form walk so last minute..."

Miss Henderson did not bother to reply to this. Then there was the slam of a door, and she was gone, leaving rolling, hiccuping sobs behind. The four children looked at each other in silence.

Freya took her ear from the wall. She didn't want to hear Henny crying. She hadn't believed the kindly mistress had the greed or the nerve for a theft like this, and she was right. It had been her *sister's* plan, not hers.

"The crying one is the thief from the museum," said Daniel. "The other one is your headmistress, right?"

"Yep," Freya said. Daniel's instinctual mistrust of Miss Henderson had been correct. She had been running the show, even while she herself was safely tucked away in Sodden-Under-Foot. Freya wondered what debt poor Henny owed her.

But there were more pressing questions to settle. She turned to Abigail.

"You know we're not the thieves now," she said. "Do you still want to tell Miss Henderson about us?"

Abigail was chewing on the end of her ponytail, with an expression on her face that Freya had never seen before. It was uncertainty. Slowly, she said, "I know what it sounded like – but – there must be another explanation."

"Oh really?" said Freya. "Do you have one?"

Abigail was silent.

"Abigail, we *were* in the museum that night," said Freya, "and Daniel saw someone else there. We've been investigating, and everything we've found out points to Henny. I'm sorry, but this is *exactly* what it sounds like." And she found, to her surprise, that she *was* sorry. Evidently, Henny had been pushed into this. Catching her out gave Freya no satisfaction.

"The rules. . ." said Abigail quietly. "Trespassers . . . it's in chapter nine." Then, more certainly, "And I'm *head girl*."

Freya could see that thinking outside the rule book was going to take Abigail a minute. After all, she *had* been at the school since she was very small. She had learned the rule book alongside counting and the alphabet.

"Come on, Abigail," said Freya. "I know you don't like me. But that's not important any more. You know who the thieves are now. You *wouldn't* hand us over to Miss Henderson. Would you?"

There was a long silence. But at last, Abigail said: "No."

For now, then, she was on their side. Or at least not against them.

Before Freya could respond, Esmie cleared her

throat. She jabbed her finger at the wall, towards where Henny sat crying, and said, "We should talk to her."

The others raised their eyebrows in unison.

"But Esmie, what if—" started Freya.

"But supposing she—" began Daniel.

Through her ponytail, Abigail began to murmur that trespass in the headmistress's office would be ten demerits.

"*Listen*," demanded Esmie – and they did.

On the other side of the wall, Henny sobbed and sobbed. The sobs were more heartbreaking now than before, a full-scale flood of horror and regret. Slowly, Freya nodded. Daniel nodded. Abigail carried on wibbling her head and chewing her hair, which was going to have to do, because they weren't going to get much else out of her right now.

Esmie felt the edges of the wood for the catch, and the children slid open the portrait of Lord Throgmorton in Miss Henderson's office, and began climbing out one by one.

Henny looked up from her hankie in red-eyed astonishment.

"Oh!" she exclaimed. "Freya – and Abigail! And who are you two?" She opened and shut her mouth, twice; then opened it again, to conclude, "Oh *dear.*"

No wonder Henny had been so surprised. Walls, to humans, are solid. People are not supposed to come crawling through them.

This is, however, a matter of perspective. There was a beetle who lived in a crack in that particular wall. It was a small crack, but to the beetle, it was a great valley. For him, that solid wall was a craggy thing – a landscape of hills and ravines and strange, looming shadows. That wall, to him, was the whole world.

He had no idea about the humans climbing through his wall. After all, that was happening inches and inches away.

The Throgmorton thief

"Where did you. . .?" said Henny.

"There are secret passages," said Freya. "It's a long story."

Henny's eyes were wide with fright. The twins stared back at her with enormous solemnity. She hiccuped at them uncertainly.

"Don't cry, miss," said Freya. It was strange to see a teacher crying. "We'll help."

This set Henny off into new peals of sobs, during which she mumbled that they didn't know, and they couldn't help, and she didn't deserve, and there wasn't any way anyone could anyway.

"We *do* know," said Freya. "And we might be able to help. We know where Miss Henderson put the Dragons, for a start."

But Henny was crying too hard to listen. In the end Esmie sighed, climbed back into the tunnel, came back out again with a Dragon, and put it down in front of her.

Henny stared. Her sobbing slowed to a confused sort of hiccuping. "Where did you. . .?"

"In the secret tunnels behind the painting," said Freya. "They're all there. That's what we were trying to say."

Henny gazed at the Dragon. It gazed haughtily back. But just as she seemed to be about to stop crying, the door opened, and Mrs Clod appeared with a hoover.

Everyone turned to look at her. Henny covered the Dragon with her cardigan.

"I hoover the headmistress's office at ten thirty," explained Mrs Clod; and she plugged her hoover in and switched it on.

"COULD WE JUST HAVE A MINUTE, MRS CLOD?" shouted Freya.

"I HOOVER AT TEN THIRTY," replied Mrs Clod.

"I CAN SEE THE DRAGON, CLARISSA, STOP RUINING A PERFECTLY GOOD CARDIGAN."

Henny meekly uncovered the Dragon and gazed uncertainly at Mrs Clod. She looked how Freya felt. It was difficult to think while the hoover roared.

And then, as though they were locked in a looping nightmare, the door opened again. Miss Richards's neat head appeared around the door. She said, "MRS CLOD, COULD I—" and then, seeing the others, "OH, SORRY TO—" and then, seeing the Dragon, "UM."

Mrs Clod switched the hoover off and faced them all, hands on hips, wellies akimbo. "Is there any reason," she demanded, "why the whole world has descended on this study when it's time for me to hoover?"

There was silence. Miss Richards looked stunned. Henny was whimpering. The twins were staring at Mrs Clod. Freya found herself exchanging glances with Abigail for the third time, this time with eyebrows raised slightly, as though they were sharing a joke – then Abigail caught herself and scowled.

"Come in and shut the door," Mrs Clod said to Miss Richards. "Do you want the whole world to see that thing?" She bent down to turn on the hoover again, but just then there were hurried footsteps, and Miss Featherly's voice could be heard from behind Miss Richards, even more breathlessly emotional than usual.

"Is the headmistress there?" she panted. "It's urgent. My room has been *robbed*." And she pulled the door open wider, pushing past the history mistress, a look of outrage on her face.

She stopped. She took in the assembled scene, Dragon and hoover and all. After a moment, she said, "Oh."

Miss Richards looked out into the entrance hall nervously, to check nobody else had seen; then she shut the door. "Right," she said.

"Everybody get in one corner, please," said Mrs Clod. "You're cluttering up the carpet. I don't even know who you two *are*," she added, pointing the nozzle at the twins.

So Freya introduced the twins, which didn't clear up much, while everyone else carried on gaping at each other in amazement and cluttering up the carpet as much as ever.

"Mrs Clod," said Henny. Her voice was still thick with hiccups, but surprisingly determined. "Would you be so kind as to delay the hoovering for a moment? I would like to say something."

Mrs Clod sighed, and said, "Ten thirty's when I hoover." But she abandoned the hoover at last, and sat in the windowsill to wait, arms folded. A hush fell over the group as Henny took deep, shuddering breaths. Miss Richards walked over to the other chair and sat down; Miss Featherly fluttered nervously by the door; the twins settled back to back on the floor; and Freya and Abigail perched on the desk.

At last, Henny spoke.

"I don't want any of you to get in trouble," she said. "I think you should all leave before anybody finds you here with – with *this*." She looked at Freya. "And you don't have to worry any more, Freya. I'm going to confess. You see" – Henny looked miserably at the floor – "*I* stole the Dragons."

"I know," said Miss Richards.

"Yes, so do I," said Miss Featherly.

"So do we," said Freya, and the twins nodded

gravely, while Abigail continued to chew her ponytail in silence.

"And so do I," said Mrs Clod. "Can I hoover now?"

"Just a moment," said Miss Richards. "We need to talk about this. Could we put the Dragon away somewhere safe, please? Does anybody know where Miss Henderson is?"

"She's in town," said Henny numbly. As she spoke, Esmie stood, and took the Dragon to the painting. She slid it aside, and climbed through to put it back in its hiding place. Miss Richards's mouth fell open in surprise; Miss Featherly gasped; Mrs Clod blinked a bit before recovering, and muttering that she wasn't cleaning in *there* as well, there was already far too much to do, and heavens knew she wasn't paid enough.

Henny was still looking from face to face in confusion at the revelation that her secret was, in fact, not very secret at all.

"How did you all know?" she said. "That I did it, I mean?"

Everyone looked at each other for a moment.

"Well," said Miss Richards, "the day the bat was

found, I went up into the attic, to check for any more. A bunch of keys up there caught my eye while I was looking – big old-fashioned keys, but shining like they were brand new – but I didn't really think anything of it until the next day. When DI North arrived and I saw Dr Robinson's keys, the similarity was obvious. I went back up to look, but they were gone. I assume you took them away and hid them, Clarissa?"

Henny shook her head, wide-eyed. "That was Annabel. I put the keys up there, along with the sketches I used to make them, which was *s-silly* of me. The sketches fell on Annabel during all the ruckus with the bat, and she was ever so cross . . . said it was a terrible hiding place. . ." She wiped her face on her sleeve. "She said she'd hidden them somewhere else, somewhere better; and I had to tell her then that the keys were up in the attic too. She m-must have gone back for them."

Miss Richards passed Henny a box of tissues, and gave her a little pat on the arm, before resuming her story. "Well, she stumped me there, all right. But I knew what I'd seen. My first thought was Mrs Clod, since she cuts all the school's keys. I peeped in her cupboard the next day, and found a series of extraordinary sketches for what looked like keys to all of the Throgmorton's buildings – and most tellingly of all, three keys for the school! So I took them. But when I confronted her, she told me *her* story. . ." And she nodded to Mrs Clod, handing the explanation over.

"I was fixing up the portrait that the bat flew into," Mrs Clod explained. "I tried to get it off the wall, and discovered a sort of hole behind it – another of those blessed tunnels, I suppose. The sketches were in there, in an old envelope addressed to Clarissa. Must've been where the headmistress hid them. I thought it was more letters." She turned to Henny. "I realized a few months ago, Clarissa, that the Society was replying to all your submissions; but your sister was throwing their letters away."

Henny's mouth fell open at this, but Mrs Clod rolled on regardless.

"I rumbled her a couple of months back, when I found a whole bunch of your letters in the bin, and started to keep an eye out for what was happening.

They've been getting more and more interested in your work – which spooked her, I guess. Anyway, I started fishing them out and getting them through to you once I realized. A good thing too, or you'd never have got your acceptance letter. I assumed those sketches were more letters – but of course, it turned out to be you, using an old envelope."

Henny's mouth was still open in astonishment. She looked as though she wanted to speak, but nothing came out. She just stared, wide-eyed, at Mrs Clod.

"So, anyway," said Miss Richards, after a moment's pause. "Mrs Clod says she lets you borrow her tools sometimes for your work – so when she saw the sketches she put two and two together and guessed that you'd used the key cutter. Right?"

"Right," said Henny weakly.

"So," said Miss Richards, "that accounts for *us*. But I don't know about *you*, Lillian?"

Miss Featherly looked a little sheepish. She cleared her throat. "Well, I borrowed your binoculars to go bat-watching, Clarissa. And when I held them up to my eyes, I saw the image of three locks on there, one above the other. I didn't realize quite what I was looking at until the next day. When DI North was interviewing me about my whereabouts that night, she mentioned the mystery of the three locks on the school's Dragon – the only locks that Dr Robinson's keys couldn't account for.

"I'd seen you out and about, that night, you see," she added, to Henny. "So I looked again at that picture, and began to piece things together. But now the binoculars and a – er – letter, are missing from my study."

"It's OK," said Freya. "*We* took them."

"She was going to blackmail you," said Daniel helpfully to Henny. "That's what was in the letter."

"But," said Miss Featherly with great dignity, "I changed my mind."

"Blackmail, Lillian?" said Miss Richards coldly, looking pointedly at the ruby Miss Featherly was wearing at her neck. "I didn't realize you were so short of cash."

Miss Featherly was silent.

"She didn't want money," Daniel chimed in. "The letter said she wanted Henny to keep her secret."

"What secret?" said Henny.

Miss Featherly went bright pink. "It was nothing. Nothing important," she said.

The others all just looked at her, waiting.

"Look," she said. "All it was," she said; then, "I only..."

Everyone else continued to look.

Miss Featherly took a deep breath, then continued in a much smaller voice, very fast. "I've written some books. They're rather successful. Millicent Leatherby the Space-Cowgirl Detective. But they're the most terrible rubbish, and I still want to be taken seriously as a poet one day. So I'm writing under a false name. I thought Clarissa was hinting that she knew, and I panicked."

Freya remembered Miss Featherly's outrage on the stairs, when Henny had brought up the Millicent Leatherby books. It felt like a lifetime ago. Lillian Featherly: Millicent Leatherby. It wasn't exactly imaginative.

"Writing successful books is nothing to be ashamed of," said Miss Richards.

"I don't know," said Mrs Clod, "I read one once. Some bits are *naughty*. Like when—"

"They're just not *highbrow*," cut in Miss Featherly quickly. "If anybody knew, my *real* work would never be taken seriously. I'm very embarrassed about them – but they do earn a nice little income."

So that was how Miss Featherly had so many nice things, Freya thought; she was earning on the side with her books. She remembered the locked drawer full of Miss Featherly's writing: a different secret entirely. So many secrets. She suddenly felt very tired.

Henny, meanwhile, was staring at Miss Featherly in wonder. "You write the Millicent Leatherby books?" she said. "But they're wonderful!"

Miss Featherly flushed again. "Thank you," she said, looking quite pleased. She turned to Freya and said a little too loudly, "And how did *you* come to be involved in all this? Why were your keys outside the museum?"

"We were there that night," said Freya. "The twins needed to check on one of the missing bats, and it lives there. So we were following the bats as well. Just like the rest of you."

A strange feeling crept over her. Seven roosts disturbed; seven humans brought to the thief. She didn't believe that the seven Dragons really came with guardian spirits and a curse, of course. Those were just old legends. But still.

There was no time to dwell on it. She told their story, right up to Abigail following them into the tunnel. When she had finished, there was a short silence.

It was Henny who broke it, with a loud sniff. "Well, it sounds like you all know most of it then." She wiped her face with her cardigan sleeve, and sat up a little straighter. "Yes, I made those keys. I took the Dragons."

"But Clarissa, *why?*" said Miss Richards. "I should have gone to DI North straight away, but I've been holding out. I couldn't quite believe it."

Henny flapped her cardigan helplessly. "I needed to pay my debt," she said. "This was the only way."

"A debt? Clarissa, I think you'd better start from the beginning," said Miss Richards, gently.

From the faraway look in Henny's eyes, Freya got the impression that the *real* beginning might be a long way off, in the unfathomable land of the Henderson sisters' childhood. But she started, mercifully, closer to home. "I . . . make things. Little experiments and inventions. I always write them up and send them to the Society, even though they aren't any good. But a few months ago something rather . . . well, rather wonderful happened." She went slightly pink. "They accepted one of my inventions – my sonoscopes. They're a new kind of sonar device, they create very precise images using sound waves, it took me *years* – anyway. The Society built a pair using my blueprints, and put them in the Higgs-Harriot Hall and – well, they said they were going to make me a Fellow!"

So they really were her invention. Henny had always seemed so silly, with her *oh dear*ing and her staring eyes – but she was clever underneath it all, in her own way. All of her late-night experiments had paid off.

Henny went on. It seemed to be a relief to talk, now she had started. "I was so happy. But when I told Annabel. . . Oh, dear. Well, you might know that some years ago there was an incident with an experiment of mine and a little, ah, explosion. I did quite a lot of damage to the building, and some valuable paintings."

"She was very good about it. To protect me she paid for the damage herself straight away. She's been taking my salary over the years to pay it back, but I hadn't finished paying yet, and of course if I leave the school I will have to start paying for rent and food and everything else she gives me for free, and I won't be able to give her any more. So I – I couldn't leave." Henny paused to hiccup into her hankie. "Then when Annabel saw the sonoscopes – well, it gave her an idea. She figured out how I could pay her back. I could have my dream *and* be a Fellow." She blew her nose, and added miserably, "She's risking ever such a lot for me. She's going to arrange the sale of the Dragons. All I had to do was go out and sonograph each of the locks earlier this week, then make keys and take the statues. She's very patient. She's even going to help me rehearse what to say to the detective tomorrow, once everyone is in bed. She's really been wonderful. And as soon as this is all over and my debt is paid, she's going to announce my new appointment as a Fellow, and let me leave."

Everyone else looked at each other, as Henny buried her face in her hands and took some deep breaths.

Miss Henderson certainly didn't *sound* like she'd been wonderful.

"But everything went wrong," Henny said. "Your keys were found, Freya, and everyone suspected you. I feel just t-terrible. We couldn't get rid of the Dragons, with the police watching. And then when my sonoscopes went missing . . . oh, goodness, I was sure that someone was on to me. . ." And at this Henny began to dissolve again, and although she kept talking, it because increasingly impossible to make out any words.

"Well, don't fret about it now, Clarissa, we've found them again," said Miss Richards. "But for heaven's sake, those paintings you blew up were really nothing very special; and the damage to the room was bad, but it wouldn't take *years* of your salary to repay. You must have covered your debt a long time ago by now."

Henny gaped at her. "But – but Annabel said. . ."

"I think," said Miss Richards firmly, "that your sister might not always tell you the truth, Clarissa."

"Of course she doesn't," said Mrs Clod. "She just doesn't *want* you to be a Fellow. That's why she took all your post. She can't bear to think of you rising above her."

"I still can't quite believe. . . Annabel wouldn't. . ."

"If you don't believe me," said Mrs Clod, "ask the girl doing an impression of a dead fish." And she jerked her head at Abigail, who had turned a little pale; and her mouth hung open, ponytail forgotten.

"I didn't know, I swear," she said. "But Miss Henderson had me bring her any letters of yours from the post tray – she just said she was handling them for you. Said you lost track of them otherwise. I didn't question it."

"You wouldn't know a question if it bit you on the backside," said Mrs Clod.

"*Thank* you, Mrs Clod," Miss Richards cut in. "Clarissa, it does sound like your sister has been deliberately holding you back. And taking your salary, all these years. . ."

"It's not like that! She *needed* me to pay her back, she couldn't spare it . . . she showed me letters from the bank, she's still in a *lot* of debt."

Miss Richards rolled her eyes. "I'm not surprised.

She was so sure she was going to win the prize money that she spent it all ahead of time. You know that Throg Three had as good as promised her the Lifetime Service Award this year – and then the seventh Dragon was found. She's been furious ever since, as poor Freya here can testify."

So it was Miss Henderson, not Miss Richards, who was jealous of her dad. Freya had misunderstood Miss Richards' meaning, when she had said that some people might envy him. No wonder the headmistress had always been so spiteful to Freya.

"She was going to retire," supplied Mrs Clod. "I saw her resignation letter one time when I was cleaning, all ready to go. I wondered why she never handed it in. But if she's really got all this debt to pay off, I guess she's stuck working here now." And she chuckled to herself, as though this was quite a good joke.

Miss Richards looked less amused. "I can just imagine her satisfaction," she said grimly. "Taking His Lordship's finest treasure from him – the very treasure that took her prize money from under her nose – and living for life on the riches. This was about her greed, Clarissa, and her pride too – but not your debt." She reached out to put a hand on Henny's shoulder. "I'm sorry."

Henny sniffed an enormous sniff, and gazed round at them all, as though looking for someone to say it wasn't true. Freya looked at her feet.

"Right," said Mrs Clod. "Have we cleared everything up yet? Can I hoover?"

"Just a minute," said Miss Richards. She pulled herself up very straight, and her voice was firm. They all turned to look at her. "We have to decide what to do."

"*Do?*" faltered Henny.

"Well, it's clear that DI North still considers Freya to be the key suspect. I imagine she'll be under pressure to push forward with that line of enquiry, now that Throg Three is involved. Apparently the police have a witness who says Freya wasn't in bed on the night of the theft."

At this, Mrs Clod gave Abigail another pointed look, and the girl buried her head in her hands. "I'm sorry, Freya," she said. "I was awake early – I have trouble sleeping sometimes – and I saw you coming back in the morning, from my window. I thought – I thought I was being good."

"I'll confess," said Henny, with sudden determination. Her face was pale and set. She stood up. "I'll confess *right now.*"

She squared her shoulders and stepped towards the door, but Mrs Clod brandished the hoover nozzle menacingly, blocking her path.

"Now hold on. You've spent your whole life under the thumb of that sister of yours, and this is your chance to break free. You aren't going to throw that chance away until you have to." She thrust her face close to Henny's. "Use that brain of yours, Clarissa. There must be another way."

Even though Freya had spent the last three days trying to find the thief so she could hand them over to DI North, now that the moment was finally here, she found that she agreed with Mrs Clod. The thought of Henny in prison was heartbreaking. Freya watched her, worrying at her buttons and gazing at them all helplessly, and wondered who Henny might have been without a lifetime of bullying from her sister. She hadn't stood a chance.

"Could we just ... put the Dragons somewhere ... to be found again?" said Abigail.

Henny shrugged helplessly. "I don't know if that will mean the investigation is over. Throg Three's on the warpath."

Miss Richards nodded. "It certainly wouldn't be the end of the matter, I'm afraid. There'll have to be an answer."

"Frame someone?" suggested Mrs Clod.

"Never!" declared Henny, and began charting her course for the door again. "No one else must be arrested for this. Never! I'll confess—"

"Wait," said Freya. She said it with such sudden excitement that everyone really did wait exactly where they were, cardigans and hoovers aloft, faces eager.

"We *could* frame someone," she said slowly. "In a way. Someone who wouldn't be arrested, because only *humans* can be arrested."

Everyone stared at her blankly, except Daniel and Esmie, whose eyes lit up.

Freya felt unexpected laughter bubbling up inside. It was time, she thought, to make the universe look a lot more magical and mysterious than anyone had bargained for.

"Maybe," she said, "it would be a good idea for everyone if that nice PC Fig turned out to be right after all. Maybe this *was* all the work of those thieving Throgmorton bats."

For a moment, the humans were silent.

They did things with the muscles in their faces, like drawing them together on the forehead, or pulling them upwards at the corner of their mouths.

Their breathing changed – faster or slower or heavier or lighter.

They sat differently, leaning forward, or huddling in on themselves, or slumping thoughtfully.

Freya read all these things, without even realizing she was doing it. She knew that the twins quite liked her idea, and Miss Richards was a bit worried about it, and Mrs Clod was amused, and Henny was too unhappy to even hold it straight in her head. She knew all that without anybody speaking, which is quite like the bees dancing, and really very clever.

She didn't know what Abigail was thinking. Some humans are harder to read this way than others.

The thieving
Throgmorton bats

It took a while to convince everyone.

"It's a great idea," said Daniel, and Esmie nodded. Freya gave them a grateful look. But Miss Richards said she wasn't sure, and Miss Featherly went a little faint at the very thought, and Mrs Clod tapped Freya on the head with her hoover nozzle and rolled her eyes.

Freya was insistent. "PC Fig is searching the roosts tomorrow morning," she said. "He's been looking forward to it all weekend. He's sure the bats were behind the thefts. Well, we'll prove him right. We'll leave a Dragon in each one."

"They won't buy it," said Miss Richards. "Well," she amended, "PC Fig might. But DI North isn't stupid."

Freya was trying not to think about DI North. "It's worth a shot," she said. "If DI North doesn't believe it, *then* you can tell the truth, Henny. But we should try, at least."

"Yes – let's try," said Henny. The sudden, desperate hope on her tearful face was almost harder to look at than the crying had been. "You know, PC Figs's calculations *do* actually add up – it wouldn't be *impossible* for the bats to carry the Dragons. I shall put the Dragons in the roosts myself – oh." Her face fell again. "I'm meant to be meeting Annabel at midnight. We were going to practise my story for the police."

"You'll have to go," Freya said. "If you cancel on Miss Henderson she'll get suspicious – I bet you've never said no to her about anything."

She hadn't spoken harshly, but Henny's eyes widened, as though she was registering for the first time that this was true; and she nodded.

"You can't do it, then," said Freya. "I will."

"Us too," said the twins.

"And me," said Abigail, through a mouthful of ponytail. She lifted her chin. "To make up for the letters. And . . . everything."

"It's a ridiculous plan," said Mrs Clod. "I'm in."

"And I," declared Miss Featherly nobly, standing up to add to the drama of it.

"Oh – all right," agreed Miss Richards. "It's worth a try."

"Seven of us," said Freya. "Seven Dragons, seven roosts. We've got Henny's keys to all of them. Daniel and Esmie, can you draw everyone maps to find the bats?"

The twins said that they could. They all agreed to meet at midnight. Until then, there was nothing to do but wait – and Miss Henderson would be back soon, so as Miss Richards pointed out, they would have to do their waiting somewhere else.

Daniel and Esmie went back behind the painting, to hide in Lord Throgmorton's study. The others went back out into the entrance hall one by one, except Mrs Clod, who was finally able to hoover.

Girls at Throgmorton's had free time on Sunday

afternoons, but the next task on Freya's list of punishments was to spend the afternoon with Miss Timms writing lines. She sat in a dim classroom, writing *I must not disgrace my school* until her hand ached. Normally Freya hated lines: it seemed such a waste to think one thought over and over again, when there were so many others to be thought. But today all her thoughts were jumpy, and it was quite soothing. She tried to concentrate on the curling flow of ink, and the ache in her hand, and nothing else.

It half worked.

She could barely eat dinner, meagre as it was. Abigail left her plate untouched. Although they didn't say a word to each other, or even *look* at each other, Freya felt tied to her by an invisible string all through the meal. The chatter and laughter around them seemed to be coming from a different world.

The bell went for bed. All the girls went upstairs in a normal, going-to-bed-on-a-Sunday way; except two, who did their best impression of it. Miss Richards paced her classroom; in her study, Henny was going over a lifetime of memories of her sister, and rethinking them all, which made her heart do strange somersaults between freedom and heartache; in the hallway outside, Mrs Clod dusted lanterns and hummed to herself. Beneath the surface of the school, two wide-eyed children huddled together on the floor of Lord Throgmorton's secret study, drawing maps in neat black ink.

At midnight, Freya slipped out of bed, and went to Henny's study.

Mrs Clod and Miss Richards were already there, Miss Richards looking pale and anxious, Mrs Clod doing a crossword.

"Hi," Freya whispered.

Mrs Clod waved cheerfully, and Miss Richards murmured, "Hello, Freya. Ready?"

"Ready," said Freya. It was more or less true.

Abigail was the next to arrive, and she and Freya exchanged awkward little *hello*s – not quite friendly, but not unfriendly either. The twins clambered out through the portrait moments later, bearing keys and maps and the first of the dragons; they had to go back a few more times to bring the rest. Then they were only waiting for Miss Featherly.

They waited.

They continued to wait.

"Bet she's bailed," said Daniel.

But she had not. She arrived late, looking worryingly faint, and muttering poetic lines about Bravery in the Face of Danger; but she came. That made seven.

Freya handed out keys, Dragons and maps. She gave Miss Featherly the school's Dragon. If she was going to faint, Freya reasoned, it had better be on the school premises.

To be on the safe side, the rest of them agreed to leave the school by the twins' secret passage. They crept down the snitching staircase, through the stony silence of the dining hall, and down through a floorboard to the cellars below. Six torches came on, and bobbed through the darkness, up the slope of the coal cellar, out into the street beyond the school.

Rain and fog had both gone. The night was clear and bitter.

"Good luck, everyone," whispered Freya. The others all whispered good luck at once, like wind through ivy, before going their separate ways.

Esmie and Freya started out in the same direction. They walked quickly, heads bowed against a cold wind.

"Freya," said Esmie quietly, "do *you* think with the seven roosts waking up, and the seven of us all being led here by the bats, this is something to do with the seven guardian spirits? That's what Daniel thinks. He thinks something horrible must be going to happen to Miss Henderson now."

"No," said Freya. "I think Henny woke the bats up with the sonoscopes. And we all just – bumbled into the middle of Miss Henderson's mess."

Esmie sighed. "You're right. It just *feels* more magical than that."

Freya didn't reply. She didn't know how to put into words what she felt: that the invisible echoing world of the bats was enough by itself. It didn't need a myth to make it magical.

They parted at the corner of the street, with Esmie turning off for the theatre. Freya had the key to the museum. It was lonely without Esmie, and she ran all the way.

The lawn outside the museum was caked with frost,

and it crackled under her feet. It was strange to be here alone, on a night so brim-full of stillness. The Dragon was heavy in her satchel.

At the door, she put the key in the lock, and turned.

The same old shadows and silence waited. They filled up the whole world with their strangeness.

"Hello," she whispered to the mummies. "Nice to see you again." Saying it made her feel just a *little* bit friendlier towards them.

She pattered up the wide stone steps, through to the creaking back staircase, up to the storage room. The dust sheets loomed like badly formed ghosts. Freya set her torch on the floor, where it wouldn't shine on the windows or wake Nimrod; then she turned on the light, and found the little bundle of bat.

"Hello," she whispered. "Sorry to disturb you."

Nimrod hung silently, magnificently undisturbed. One wing was slightly crooked.

She took the Dragon out of its bag and arranged it on a beam next to the bat. It was the smallest statue, suitable for a one-bat roost, and she thought it seemed friendly – there was a hint of a smile to its mouth. "This is for you," she said to Nimrod. "If anyone asks, you stole it, OK?"

Nimrod did not express an opinion.

"Thanks," said Freya.

For a moment, one of the bat's eyes seemed to flicker open, and wink shut again. But maybe it was a trick of the light.

Freya took one last look at the bat and the ivory Dragon. Then she picked up her torch and wound back down, down the creaking back staircase, down the wide stone steps, past the mummies, through the door and out on to the frosted grass.

Even with the door shut, the shadows and silence were there. Just beneath the surface. She ran all the way back to school.

The fox was disturbed again. He heard the crunch of the grass, a silvery, crackling sound; and the heavy breathing, a whooshing sound; and the fall of the footsteps, a great drumbeat. He trotted out of the way, and watched from behind a bush as Freya charged past.

What were the humans up to these days?

The wisdom of PC Fig

The next day, lessons at Throgmorton's School for Girls were cancelled. They had a party to prepare for.

Miss Henderson set everyone to work with something almost like glee. This was, Freya supposed, her big triumph. A party for Dr Robinson and his Dragons, with no Dragons in sight.

Freya was assigned to hanging bunting in the entrance hall, which was good, because it meant she could keep an eye on the front door, and be the first to know if PC Fig arrived. Abigail was there too, and the invisible thread was still there between them. Freya always knew where she was, in amongst the forest of bunting. She noticed that Miss Richards, Miss Featherly, Henny and Mrs Clod had all found themselves jobs to do out here as well.

Had PC Fig gone to check the roosts yet? When would they know?

The first time there was a thumping on the front door it sent her heart *thlop-thutter*ing so much that she nearly stumbled off her stepladder. It turned out to be a marching band who had been hired for the occasion, but after that, her heart kept up the pattering.

The second thump was Throg Three, and Miss Henderson came oozing out to meet him.

"Your Lordship," she said, "welcome. Everything is progressing wonderfully."

"Is it?" He regarded her with contempt. "I don't see my Dragons."

"*Such* a shame," she said, smiling a bright little smile. "It does seem as though the police are stumped. I do hope the guests won't mind."

"Mind?" Throg Three turned gently purple. "*Mind?* People are coming from all over the world to see them! Of course they will mind. Do you realize what this means for the reputation of my Trust?"

"*Such* a shame," Miss Henderson repeated. "By the way, Your Lordship, I'm sorry if this is a bad time, but I wanted to give you notice. I plan to retire."

Freya tried to look interested in her bunting. *So*, Miss Richards and Mrs Clod had been right about that, then! Now that she had stolen herself a comfortable fortune to retire on, Miss Henderson couldn't wait to get out of Throgmorton's.

Throg Three just blinked at her. "Retire?" he repeated.

"With immediate effect," said the headmistress, still smiling. "I will leave the school tomorrow, I'm afraid. I *do* hope that doesn't add to your troubles."

"Tomorrow?" He spluttered. "Quite impossible, Miss Henderson, I haven't got time right now to be replacing—"

"I'm afraid," said Miss Henderson, "that I am not willing to negotiate on this matter. Your *Lordship*." And she went sailing off to the other side of the hall with triumphant dignity, Throg Three gaping after her. She was so busy sailing that she knocked into Quiet Carol, who wobbled and got a bit tangled up in her bunting;

but she didn't let this trouble her, and went gliding onwards to oversee the cupcake arrangements on the other side of the hall.

Freya was still untangling Quiet Carol when PC Fig finally arrived, with DI North in tow. His face was flushed pink with excitement. The detective's face gave nothing away.

"Aha!" cried Throg Three. "Detective! You're late. Have you done anything useful yet?"

DI North eyed Throg Three thoughtfully. Her face *mostly* continued to give nothing away, but Freya caught a slight flicker which seemed to suggest that she didn't think very much of Lord Joseph Edward Throgmorton the Third.

"Good morning," she said. "Apologies for the delay. It was in a good cause – I was called out by PC Fig here because he recovered the Dragons this morning."

Freya tried to remember what "surprised and curious" looked like, and made her face do that. Miss Richards, she noticed, took a sudden studious interest in the nearest flower arrangement, while Henny was actually shaking.

Miss Henderson sped over from the cupcake stand. She looked at the detective in horror.

"R-recovered?" she whispered.

"Well?" demanded Throg Three. "Where were they? Who was responsible?"

"It appears," said DI North, her voice carefully even, "that PC Fig was quite correct." PC Fig beamed at everyone, while Miss Henderson's badly hidden horror slid slightly into badly hidden confusion. "The statuettes," the detective went on, "have been located in several bat roosts around the city. It seems that most of the bats, er, worked in groups; one larger bat which lives alone sustained an injury to its left wing, and may have attempted to carry a statuette by itself. At any rate, it appears that PC Fig was right. The bats are our culprits."

Across the hall, Freya caught Abigail's eye, then quickly looked away again. She knew that there had been well over a hundred million billion seconds since the beginning of planet earth, but she thought the second that followed DI North's announcement had to be the longest. The entrance hall was utterly silent, apart from the merry fluttering of bunting.

Then Throg Three inflated his lungs to their full capacity, and roared: "BATS?"

This was slightly ruined by the marching band choosing this moment to kick off their rehearsal. They came stepping smartly into the hall, playing the school song at top volume. It took a good few minutes for PC Fig to convince them to stop, and persuade the band leader that now really wasn't a good moment.

"Rehearsal time was in our contract," said the band leader.

"Yes, I quite understand," said PC Fig. "But we're just announcing the discovery of a crime ring of treasure-hunting bats."

"We could play the *Batman* theme tune?" suggested a tuba player hopefully. PC Fig looked quite tempted, but DI North firmly declined; and the band trooped off to rehearse in the assembly hall instead.

"Detective," boomed Throg Three, who had been stewing in his rage through all of this, "this is an insult! Are you seriously telling me that my statues were removed by some flying rodents? Have you arrested them?"

"Bats aren't actually rodents," said PC Fig.

"I don't *actually* care!" snarled Throg Three. "Arrest them!"

With an extra-neutral face, DI North said, "There aren't any laws that would allow us to arrest bats."

"Their owners, then!"

"Nobody owns them."

Throg Three snorted. "*Somebody* must own them. Things can't just go around not being owned by anyone."

"I can assure you," said DI North patiently, "that nobody owns these bats." *They just happen to you*, Freya thought, *like demerits and weather.*

Fortunately, a girl from the cupcake team was passing through the hall with a finished tray, so Throg Three was able to take it from her and throw it against the wall to relieve his feelings (but not before removing three to cram angrily into his mouth). The cakes hit a painting of his ancestor, who smiled at him faintly through the smear of icing.

"I am going to speak to my lawyer," he announced, spraying crumbs of righteous indignation. "I will *not* be robbed without somebody feeling the consequences. I assure you, those bats will be arrested."

Freya *thought* DI North muttered, "Good luck with that," but it was difficult to be sure, because the band had struck up again from the assembly hall. She wanted to dance along to them and never stop. It had worked. *It had worked.*

But as murmuring and cake-arranging and bunting-hanging resumed, DI North walked right over to where Freya now stood, hanging bunting next to Abigail. Freya's stomach turned right over.

"Hello, Freya," said the detective.

"Hello."

"Good news about your dad's Dragons."

"Yes."

"It's very puzzling," DI North went on – and there might *almost* have been a smile at the corner of her mouth – "because I did investigate the bats a little myself. I had an entirely different theory for why they were awake. The Society had just unveiled a very interesting new sonar invention, you know, with an intriguing link to someone at the school. I visited the roosts – but somehow, when I was up there, I didn't spot the Dragons."

"Oh," was all Freya could manage.

"Perhaps I just wasn't looking properly. Or perhaps those fabled guardian spirits sorted things out."

"Um," said Freya.

"Anyway," said DI North, "I'm very happy to consider this case closed. We won't be investigating any further. I just thought you might like to know that. And that maybe a friend of yours would like to know as well. So they can make a fresh start in peace."

"Yes," said Freya. "Thank you."

"Thank *you*," said DI North. "In my line of work, Freya, there are times when I'm very glad to be proved wrong. I might have to promote PC Fig, don't you think?"

The sparrowhawk was over the school again, watching his secret glimmering map. He felt a slight change of the wind in his feathers, and adjusted his balance.

It was time to go home.

The party

The school worked hard all day. Miss Henderson disappeared inside her office and the door remained firmly closed, but Miss Richards kept things running in her absence, and by the evening, everything looked perfect. The bunting was like a thick canopy overhead, the entrance hall had been scrubbed to perfection, and there were enough cupcakes to feed the whole school for weeks.

They all gathered in the assembly hall before the guests arrived, for Throg Three to glare at them all and bellow his thanks-for-their-work and pride-in-the-school. Miss Henderson reemerged to take her place with the other mistresses, still looking dazed, like a spider in the wreckage of its broken web.

"I have," he rumbled, when thanks-and-pride had been dealt with, "some announcements. Two of my fine staff will be leaving you, girls. Clarissa Henderson has been made a fellow of the Throgmorton Society, for her pioneering work in ultrasonic – er – waves of – ah, in science. Ahem. Please join me in congratulating her."

There was a lot of amazed murmuring, and then a lot of cheering and whistling, which took a while to die down. Miss Featherly stood on her chair to applaud, and Miss Timms played a quick impromptu fanfare on the piano, ignoring Miss Henderson glaring at her.

Henny just beamed at them all. Her cardigan was inside out, but she was full of extraordinary thoughts under the surface, so maybe the cardigan didn't matter very much.

"And your headmistress—"

At this, Miss Henderson got quickly to her feet. "Forgive me," she tinkled, "for interrupting Your Lordship, but in light of our *wonderful* news today, I have – remembered – my fondness for this school. So, I will be staying."

Throg Three turned to face her very, very slowly. He looked at her for a moment without speaking.

Then – "I'm afraid," he said, "that I am not willing to negotiate on this matter."

Miss Henderson flushed a peculiar shade of red. Her little mouth opened, but nothing came out.

Throg Three turned back to the girls, who were watching in silent fascination. "Your headmistress," he resumed, "is retiring. Miss Richards has already agreed to take her place. Perhaps we could have a round of applause for your new headmistress, girls."

The girls applauded, while Miss Henderson sat down again very slowly, and licked her lips, and tried to make sense of how everything had gone so wrong so fast.

Freya didn't believe in curses, but just for a minute, she let herself pretend.

When the assembly was over, the girls gathered in the entrance hall. The marching band struck up at seven o'clock sharp, and the guests began to arrive.

There were hundreds of them. They all admired the Dragon and the bunting and so on, and tucked into the cupcakes with gusto. Miss Richards had sent a last-minute invitation to Daniel and Esmie's dad to say thank you for sorting out the bat problem. When they arrived, Freya hugged the twins very hard.

"We heard all about it from Dad – they really think it was the bats? Brilliant! Why is there so much bunting? The band's loud, aren't they?" said Daniel.

Esmie just smiled.

The staff were there too, of course, in all their finery. Mrs Clod appeared in a stunning gold ball gown over her black wellies, and Miss Featherly had prepared some poems for the occasion, which she read to anyone who would listen. Oddly, the one person who seemed genuinely captivated by them was Throg Three, who listened in magnificent silence, and coughed appreciatively after each one.

Miss Henderson was nowhere to be seen. It seemed to Freya as though the hushed atmosphere of obedience had gone too. There was a swept-clean feeling in the air. Everybody seemed giddy with it.

But there was only one person Freya was really waiting for. She peered around the room, desperate to spot him. She saw Quiet Carol and Esmie, deep in earnest conversation. She saw Henny explaining something to a wide-eyed PC Fig, and Daniel climbing on the bannister rail to get a better look at the marching band. But her dad had not arrived yet.

Abigail, as head girl, was supposed to be serving cupcakes to all the most important guests. She eyed Throg Three and Miss Featherly warily.

"I wouldn't go there," said Freya, "unless you want an earful of Miss Featherly's finest poetry."

"Freya Robinson," said Abigail. "Mockery of Miss Featherly's poetry at any time is two demerits."

Freya stared at her in amazement. "Abigail, that's not a real rule. Did you just . . . make a joke?"

Abigail shrugged. "Maybe. I doubt the old rule book applies any more. So we might as well make up our own." She held out a cupcake. "Want one?"

Freya was still licking crumbs from her fingers when the guest she had been waiting for finally arrived. He seemed to her to be the solidest, realest person in the room: like a bright home star in a sky full of distant fizzling lights.

He saw her in the same moment, and they ran to each other at once. He swept her up in an enormous hug, then set her on her feet and held her face in his hands. He looked at her, long and hard, as though he would never look away.

"Hello, Dad," she said.

"Hello, little one," he said. "Tell me. What are you thinking about?"

What had all this been like for the bat?

*It hadn't been like anything at all. Moriarty was asleep.
(Do you think bats dream in echoes?)*

*Well, fair enough. Let him sleep. It must be tiring, after
all, being a change-everything sort of bat.*

Acknowledgements

There are a lot of people who worked their magic beneath the surface of this book.

Thank you to my excellent editors, Genevieve Herr and Sophie Cashell; and the eagle-eyed copy editing of Jessica White and Pete Matthews. Thank you to my always-first and always-wise readers, Dylan Townley and Sam Plumb: you continue to be the very greatest. And thank you and KAW to Maddy Vierbuchen, for not only answering a stranger's weird questions about bats, but then sticking around afterwards to become a pal and a half. Freya would approve of this bat-based serendipity.

To the people who made this book beautiful: thank you Flavia Sorrentino for the gorgeous illustrations, and Bleddyn Sion for the exceptional design. I smile every time I look at it.

To my agent Bryony Woods, an ongoing overwhelmed thank you for making all this possible.

And to my parents, who always deserve the heartiest of thanks. THANK YOU.

When Max is sent to Istanbul to stay with her boring Great Aunt-Elodie, little does she expect to be plunged into a thrilling night-time adventure across Europe. And when the Heartbreak Diamond goes missing, Max must find her feet in a whirling world of would-be diamond smugglers, thieves and undercover detectives.

Read on for an extract…

All Max knew about her great-aunt Elodie was that she had moved to Turkey years and years ago, and that she was very rich, and lived all by herself in Istanbul. Every Christmas she sent the Morels some well-meaning but ugly knitwear, and every year they sent *her* a card with a family photo printed on the front. Apart from that, they never heard from her. She hadn't been to visit since Max was a baby.

Then one day, when December had arrived and iced Paris all over with a slippery frosting, Max skidded-slid-stumbled home from school to find her mother on the phone. She was saying "Mm-hmm, of course" with her voice, and YOU ARE AN UNBEARABLE STRAIN ON MY SAINTLY PATIENCE with her eyes. The voice tinkling on the other end was not familiar. Max made herself some hot chocolate on the stove as usual, but extra slowly and quietly, so that she could listen for clues about the mystery caller. She was curious – this was out of the ordinary, and things at her house were hardly ever out of the ordinary.

After a very long time of "mm-hmm" and "of course", her mother finally said *au revoir*, and hung up the phone. She tutted, sucked in her cheeks and rolled her eyes all at once, which made her look like an overexcited prune.

Max tipped the steaming milk out into a bowl, and cupped the bowl tightly to get some warmth back into her fingers. "Who was that, *Maman*?"

"Your great-aunt," sighed her mother. "Is that *chocolat*, Maximilienne? Don't ruin your appetite for dinner, now." (She said this every day when Max made *chocolat*. Max's house was like that: most things happened the same way every day, like gently whirring clockwork.)

"Why was she calling?" Max asked.

Max's mother sighed a second time, even more gustily. "Your great-aunt," she declared, "is a very difficult woman."

This wasn't really an answer. Max was very curious to know what made her great-aunt so difficult, but Max's mother started loudly tidying things that were already tidy, which was her way of letting Max know that she was asking too many questions. So Max took her hot chocolate, and some *tartine* to dip in it, and she went up through the house to the attic.

Max's house was full of thick curtains and dim lamps and soft carpets. It was a nice enough house, but a *heavy* sort of place. It was difficult to think anything new there, when everything was so sleepy and still and exactly-the-same-as-yesterday. Max had to find her own private places for thinking in. When she was small, she used to wriggle into a gap behind the sofa, but she couldn't fit there these days; so she had moved up into the attic instead.

No one else ever went up there. There was a skylight, and under the skylight there was an old red velvet chair that was too shabby for the rest of the house, and under the armchair there was a box of Max's notebooks. Today – like every day – she took out the latest notebook, rested the *chocolat* in the crook of her left arm, and began to write.

Max had been keeping notes for four years now. They were notes about everything that happened each day – although with things being same-as-clockwork every day there wasn't always much to report, especially during the school holidays. Max's father said that she was doing Social History, and her notes could be very important in the Future. Max's older brother

Pierre said she was being weird. Max's even older sister Claudette was much too old and important to have an opinion.

That day she made her notes, then sat and thought for a while, and watched the clouds shift over her skylight. The slice of sky above always made her feel like she could go anywhere and do anything. She forgot all about Great-Aunt Elodie's call until dinner.

The three Morel children and their parents always had dinner together, round a long table in a dark green dining room, with candles and all the right cutlery. Tonight, Max was imagining that it was the galley of a pirate ship to liven things up. She was the ship's captain, and they were going somewhere exciting, although she was a bit vague about where exactly. She gripped her sword (butter knife) fiercely, in case any of the other pirates were planning a mutiny.

"Your aunt Elodie called today," said Max's mother to Max's father. She made this sound as though it was his fault.

Max's father pulled a face. "What about?"

"Well, it's all very tiresome. Maximilienne, stop

waving your butter knife around." Max made her fierce-sword-gripping a bit subtler, and Max's mother continued. "She's rather ill, and she has to have an operation. Apparently the doctor said she ought to have someone else at home while she recovers. She was asking if one of us would like to visit." She said "visit" as though visiting would involve wading through a large swamp, covering yourself in slime, and possibly wrestling with some ill-tempered crocodiles.

As far as Max was aware, though, Great-Aunt Elodie did not live in a swamp. She lived in a big and beautiful city, far away from Paris. Max forgot all about being a pirate captain sailing to somewhere-or-other. This was better: this was real. This was the sort of thing Max always felt might happen when she looked up through the skylight, but it never had – until now.

Her mother, however, was less excited. "I'm much too busy at work," she said. "And besides –" she turned to Max's father "– she's your aunt."

But Max's father had a very important meeting with very important people coming up, and couldn't possibly go, even if it was his aunt. Max's older brother

Pierre had a national chess tournament that week, and Max's older sister Claudette had an international showjumping championship.

"Well, that's that, then," said Max's mother. "I'll just call her and tell her we can't go."

"I could go," said Max.

"She can't expect us to be at her beck and call," agreed Max's father. "We're very busy."

"I'm not busy," said Max.

"I'll just have to be firm," said Max's mother. "And we can all send her a get well soon card."

Sometimes, Max got the feeling that all the low ceilings and dim lamps and heavy curtains had cast a thick fog over her family, and they couldn't actually hear her. She tapped her mother on the shoulder. "Maman," she said, loudly, "it will be the Christmas holidays. I could go."

Max's mother and Max's father and Max's brother Pierre and Max's sister Claudette all turned to look at her, not sure what to do with this idea. Normal things for Max to do included going to school, disappearing into attics and being told off for daydreaming at the dinner table. Max going to Turkey to visit great-aunts was not on the list. Pierre snorted. Claudette examined her fingernails with magnificent disinterest.

"Don't be silly, Max," said her father. "You're only twelve."

Max was eleven, actually, but she decided not to point this out. "I'd be fine," she said. "It's not like I'd be staying by myself. I'd be with Great-Aunt Elodie."

"But it's so far away," said her mother. And she sighed despairingly at the thought of anyone being foolish enough to put a city so many miles from Paris. "It would be so tiring for you."

"I'd like to go," said Max. "Really." She tried to look sensible-and-reliable, while a great un-sensible balloon of excitement was being blown up inside her chest. To go all the way to Istanbul would be a hundred times more interesting than days and days of sitting in her attic and watching the sky and coming up with new things to pretend about the dining room. Maybe she would go on an aeroplane.

Pierre rolled his eyes. "You wouldn't like it. It won't be like one of your stupid games. You'd get homesick in three minutes."

"I wouldn't get homesick. I promise," said Max. "Please can I go?" And very subtly, just an inch, she turned her butter-knife sword on scurvy landlubber Pierre, who had already lost interest and was making a face at Claudette about something. Claudette, of course, was much too old and important to notice.

"We'll think about it," said her mother. And she started tidying the already-tidy salt and pepper shakers, so Max knew that she couldn't ask again. For the rest of dinner they talked about chess and showjumping and the neighbours, as usual; then they all had coffee and watched the evening news, as usual.

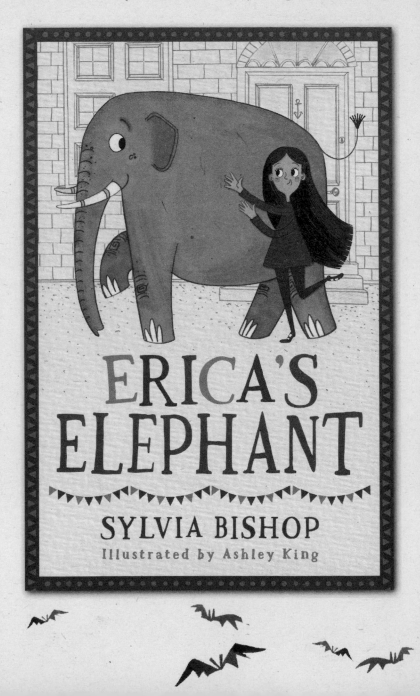

ERICA'S
ELEPHANT

SYLVIA BISHOP

Illustrated by Ashley King

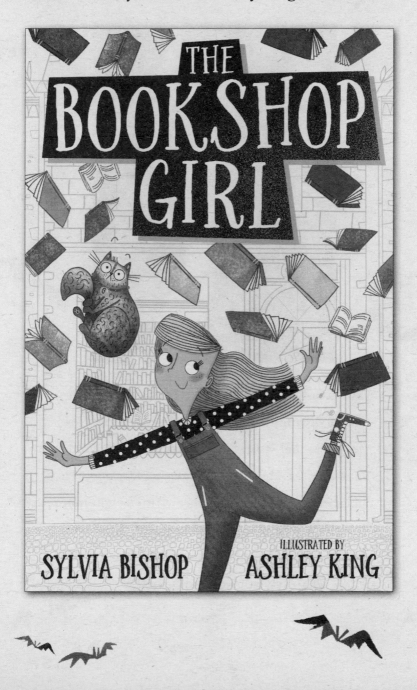

THE
BOOKSHOP
GIRL

SYLVIA BISHOP   ILLUSTRATED BY ASHLEY KING

Sylvia Bishop spent an entire childhood reading fiction, dreaming up stories and pretending. Now she writes her stories down, preferably by lamplight with tea. Her first book, *Erica's Elephant*, was published in 2016. She has since written eight more titles for young readers, and her books have been translated into sixteen languages. Find out more at sylviabishopbooks.com